CW00728420

ONE

'You could have woken me up!' I shouted at my mum.

She looked up at me from the battered sofa in the living room and grunted something about getting back late.

'Lemme sleep,' she mumbled.

'But I ain't got no money for lunch,' I told her. Only she was already asleep.

I looked around for her purse and found it lying on the floor, next to a bottle of vodka and a load of other rubbish. It was eight-thirty and I was going to be late for school again. I grabbed a fiver and ran out of the house, hoping that I wouldn't miss the eight-forty bus. I was gonna get into trouble. Again.

The bus stop was full of kids just as late as me so I stopped feeling so bad about it, wondering if my best mate Dean had walked over to our friend Grace's house, to go to school with her, which is what we did most mornings. As the bus pulled up I pushed past a load of Year Nines and paid my money.

'You wanna be careful,' said one of the older lads, Mandeep.

I looked at him and grinned. Yeah – like he was *really* scary.

'Or what?' I asked him.

'Just watch it . . .' he told me.

'Stick it,' I replied, heading upstairs to the back of the bus. Behind me I heard him ask his mates what was up with me. The knob.

It took ages to get up to Evington, where our school was, and by the time I reached the main gates, my head teacher Mr Black, was waiting for me.

'What a surprise to see you turning up late again,' he said.

'Sorry sir,' I replied, knowing that I was heading for a detention no matter what I said. No point making it harder on myself by being cheeky.

'I don't want to hear "sorry", Jit. I want to hear you saying "Good morning, Mr Black", preferably at around eight-thirty in the morning or at least by ten to nine,' he told me.

'But I was late because . . .'

Mr Black dismissed me with a wave of his hand.

'Save it, Jit. You'll need another excuse tomorrow . . .' he said.

'Knob,' I mumbled, quietly.

'With or without the "K"?' he asked me. 'Detention with a capital "D" at lunchtime, Mr Kooner. Firm but fair. Now get to your lesson before I forget that I'm in a good mood . . .'

I shrugged and walked into school, heading for my form room and my mates.

When I got there, my form teacher, Mrs Dooher, was reading out a load of messages about stuff, most of which didn't interest me at all. The only bit I caught that meant anything was about football practice being cancelled this week. I nodded at Dean, who was sitting with Grace and Hannah, another friend, one of my oldest. Next to them were Suky and Imtiaz, the other members of our little gang.

'Miss . . . !' shouted a lad called Marco. 'Jit is late again, Miss!'

Mrs Dooher looked up and smiled at me.

'Yes, Marco,' she replied. 'I can see that . . .'

'But if I was late Miss, I'd get in shit . . .' said Marco.

'MARCO!'

'Sorry Miss – I mean trouble . . .'

I glared at him. 'You'll get into trouble in a minute,' I said.

'MISS!' he squealed.

'Shut up – all of you,' Mrs Dooher said, not really shouting. She never did.

She was one of the few teachers at school who was OK. I kind of liked her and I couldn't say that about many of the others.

'Late again, bro . . .' said Dean, as I sat down between him and Grace.

'Hi Jit!' said Grace, smiling.

'All right,' I replied to both of them.

Hannah leant across Dean and whispered to me, 'You get your haircut at that new place – BlindCuts?' she asked.

'You what?' I asked.

'Your hair, Jit . . .' she told me.

I looked at Dean who shrugged.

'Hate to say it bro but you got an Afro any black man would be proud of, you get me?'

I swore and stood up, heading for the toilets.

'Sit down, Jit,' said Mrs Dooher, only I ignored her. Not because I wanted to, though. Sometimes I get so wound up that I stop hearing what people say to me. My only thought was to get to the toilets and sort out my hair so that's what I did.

Dean came in after a few minutes, as I was straightening my hair with a wet hand.

'What'd you do that for?' he asked.

'What?' I asked.

'Just walk out like that? Mrs Dooher's cool, man – she's always lookin' out for us and you just dissed her, man.'

I shrugged.

'Never meant it,' I said, feeling all bad and that.

'You is funny sometimes, bro,' said Dean.

'Whatever . . . what we got first lesson?'

Dean let up and grinned.

'English . . . not that you is gonna get nothing done. You ain't even got a pen with you . . .'

'I got up late,' I told him. 'Forgot . . .'

'You best hope Herbert ain't got another snot-filled spot on his ugly face. You know how angry he gets when his face looks like pus pizza . . .'

Herbert was an English teacher and he hated us. Not that I cared. I hated him right back, so I didn't care that he might get angry. He was a nasty man, anyway. He was always red in the face from shouting and that. And about twice a month he got these nasty boils on his face. During one lesson he had this proper beauty on his forehead. It was like another planet stuck to his head, full of pus. Halfway through the lesson he went to the toilet and squeezed it, only it started to bleed and he couldn't stop it. He came back into the lesson after five minutes and we were all messing about. When he tried to get us to calm down, we saw that the spot had gone and realised what he'd done. The whole class started laughing and he went mad. Dutty bwoi . . .

The English lesson was really boring though and

afterwards we had to stay indoors because it was raining outside. We hung out under the stairs that led to the Humanities area. There was me and Dean, Hannah and Grace. I didn't know where the other two, Imi and Suky, were but that didn't matter. It was them that we were talking about. A few weeks earlier we'd caught them walking around hand in hand and found out that they were seeing each other. For a while it was like scandal central but I didn't care about it. It wasn't like it was any of my business anyway.

'. . . And they were snogging in the Science labs,' I heard Grace saying.

'So?' asked Dean.

'Ignore him,' said Hannah. 'He's just jealous 'cause he ain't got no girl . . .'

'Me have plenty girls!' he boasted. 'I had to get rid of my phone the other day. Thing was running red hot, you get me. Pure gal a call me on it . . .'

'Yeah – like in your dreams, stinky boy,' said Grace.

'You know it's true, Sister Gee,' replied Dean.

'I heard him get a few calls,' I added, backing up my spar.

'Mostly from his mummy, tellin' him to come home for dinner,' grinned Hannah.

'Least my mum makes dinner,' countered Dean. 'You is so skinny I reckon you only eat celery or some other rabbit food . . .'

'Just 'cause you got an ass the size of London . . .' she replied.

Grace looked at me and shrugged before speaking.

'We're *supposed* to be gossiping about Imi and Suky,' she reminded us. 'Like, that's the *whole* point of being here . . .'

'I thought we was just hanging out,' I said.

'Yeah . . . we are. Hanging out and gossiping . . .' she added.

'You'll never make a girl,' Hannah told me.

'But why would I wanna be a girl?' I asked, wondering if she was going mad.

'It was a joke, Jit. You know them things that are supposed to be funny?' she told me.

'Like Hannah's hairdo. That's an example of funny, you get me?' said Dean, making me grin.

'Oh, get lost!' said Hannah. 'Come on, Grace – let's go somewhere else . . .'

'But . . .' began Grace, only Hannah ignored her and grabbed her by the arm, pulling her away.

'See you later . . .' Grace told me as she went.

'Cool,' I replied, hoping that I would.

I didn't want to go home after school, which was normal for me, and I was hoping Grace would invite me round to hers. Things were strange at home and my mum was on a bender again. She'd also taken back her old boyfriend, Micky, after kicking him out. I didn't like Micky and he didn't like me. He was a bully and the last time he'd moved in he started picking on me, calling me all kinds of names, when Mum wasn't there, and locking me out. It had got so bad that I had slept in the park for a night, until Dean's mum had spoken to my mum and sorted things out. The problem was that, with my mum, things were never sorted for long. And now he was back and making my life hell again. And that was something I could do without.

As I was thinking, Dean opened his bag and got out a load of copied CDs.

'Come, Jit – we got money to make,' he told me, handing me the copies.

We sold all kinds of things at school and had got into trouble a few weeks before with a load of dodgy mobile phones. Dean's brother Gussie always had things that he gave us to sell, mostly CDs that were burned off MP3s or pirated. Not that I was complaining. I needed the money.

'Cool – you got loads?' I asked Dean.

'Nuff . . .' he told me. 'Twelve centimetres of plastic treasure – for your musical pleasure . . .'

Dean was a wannabe rapper but sometimes his rhymes were just lame.

'How do you know that CDs are twelve centimetres anyway?' I asked him.

'I measured a few . . .' he told me, totally straight faced, like it was normal to go round with a ruler, checking the diameter of CDs. Nutter.

'Why?' I asked him.

'Why not, man?' he replied. 'Come on – let's go find Robert and Wesley, I've got some of that skater shit they like . . .'

Robert Sargeant and Wesley Magoogan were in our year and they were into fantasy novels and skater music and stuff. The school nerds. But they always bought CDs and the selection Dean had with him were exactly the sort of bands they liked.

'Cool,' I said, wondering where Grace and Hannah had gone.

TWO

Robert and Wesley were talking to some of their friends about the latest fantasy novel that they were reading. It was one of a series of books – *The Dark Lord of Hazelwitch* stories – and they had magicians and goblins and stuff in them. Exactly the sorts of books that I hated.

'The ancient flute of Kings has been taken by Bloodlehart The Great,' Robert was saying as we walked up. I swear he was just making it up though. I mean, the names were just stupid and why do all fantasy books have to have magic stones and flutes in them?

'And Princess Wondlebarn is going to have to travel back in time, to before her own birth, to save the people of Hazelwitch . . .' added Wesley as their mates stood and listened.

'But what about Gerafaggan, the dark lord?' asked Sailesh Kotecha, one of the nerd posse.

'He's takin' a break, my dan,' interrupted Dean. 'Man's got bored of being evil and that so he's doing voluntary work with the goblins . . .'

For a minute I thought that Sailesh had fallen for it, but he hadn't. Instead he tried to diss Dean.

'At least I read,' he said. 'I bet you've never even read a book from start to finish.'

Dean looked at Sailesh like he was shocked and then he looked at me with a grin.

'Read this one book,' he replied, acting serious. ''Bout how this likkle rat faced bwoi got his head mash up by me . . .'

Sailesh went red and looked down at his feet.

'You want me to finish *that* book?' asked Dean, only he didn't wait for Sailesh to answer. Instead he smiled at Robert and handed him some CDs.

'Tek a look at them, my fantasy reading brother . . . pure skate freak business, you get me? An' cheap too . . .'

Robert looked at both of us over his glasses, like we were insects or something and then he took a look at the CDs.

'WOW!' he said suddenly, pulling one out and showing it to Wesley.

'EXCELLENT!' agreed Wesley.

I looked at Dean and grinned.

'Spiffing, what?' I said, taking the mickey.

'Four pounds, man,' said Dean. 'Cheapus Maximus . . .'

'I'll take it,' said Robert, smiling, and I wondered

exactly how many Hazelwitch books there were. In the end I just asked him, as he was getting his dough out.

'Oh, there's seven so far, but that doesn't include the prequels and the two sequels that the author is writing at the same time . . .'

'You what?' I asked.

'There are going to be two *follow-up* books,' he said slowly.

I looked at him and this red haze started forming in front of my eyes. I thought he was making fun of me and I felt myself getting mad. Then, just as suddenly, I calmed down again. I would have hit him otherwise.

'I know what sequel means, you knob,' I replied. 'But how can there be two, *together*?'

Wesley took over. 'The author is writing two alternate sequels and you can choose which one suits your own taste . . .'

I thought about it for a minute.

'But if there's two sequels, with two different endings, then the next book ain't gonna make sense . . . the author's gonna have to write another two . . .' I pointed out.

Wesley grinned like he'd just been snogged by some Hollywood star.

'*Exactly* . . . and then two more and two more and . . .'

'And the whole world is gonna be full up of stupid

books about the Dutty Backside of Ganglefart . . .' said Dean, handing Robert a CD.

Wesley looked at Dean, went bright red, mumbled something about being late for lessons, and walked off. Robert looked at me and then followed his friend, as the rest of the nerd crew dispersed. I asked Dean what we had next.

'Maths,' said Dean. 'Why?'

'I don't think I'm gonna bother,' I said.

'Forget that, bro . . . you'll just get into trouble again. What's up, anyway? Things getting funny at home again?' he asked.

'NO!' I shouted.

'Easy, Jit . . . ain't no need to . . .' he began, only I didn't wait around to listen.

Instead I walked off in the direction of the main doors to the school and walked out into the rain, my head beginning to hurt. I walked around to the side of the school and into the outdoor toilets, locking myself in a cubicle. It took me a few minutes to stop feeling angry and then I started to feel stupid for shouting at my best mate and walking off. But I wouldn't have done it if he hadn't asked me about what was going on at home. It was stressful enough to deal with without having to chat about it. Only then I remembered how Dean had let me stay at his the last time things were bad, and the way his mum had sorted stuff out. I started to get angry again, this time with myself and with Micky. My head was hurting even more and I kicked at the door a few times . . .

Later on I felt all right and I found Dean and Grace in the dinner hall. They were eating and talking about Suky and Imtiaz and when I walked up, Dean just nodded at me and then told me to sit down.

'Easy bro,' he said, raising his eyebrows.

'Easy . . .' I replied.

Grace looked at us both and then began to ask a question but I jumped in.

'So what's new with the Suky an' Imi show?' I asked.

'*Well* . . .' began Grace, forgetting what she had been about to say. 'They're still being really secretive about it all. Everyone knows that they're together but they aren't telling us anything . . .'

'I can understand that,' said Dean.

'So can I,' I added, although me and Dean had different reasons.

I thought it was to do with Suky being Sikh and Imi being Muslim but Dean told Grace that the only reason they weren't saying anything was because Grace and Hannah had big gobs.

'That's not true, smelly bum,' replied Grace.

'Yeah it is,' continued Dean. 'You two are like *The Sun* and *The Mirror* combined, man, only you gossip more than even them papers . . . !'

Grace looked at me and pouted.

'Will you back me up, Jit?' she asked. 'You don't think I'm a gossip do you?'

I looked at Dean and I wanted to agree with him but I didn't want Grace to get upset so I just shrugged and said nothing. Which upset her anyway.

'Fat arse,' she said, getting up and walking off with her tray.

'Grace . . . !' I shouted after her but she just turned and stuck her tongue out at me.

'Let her go, man,' Dean told me, then he grinned. 'One of these days you an' me is gonna go over the rules when it comes to the ladies . . .'

'What . . . ?' I asked.

'You're actin' like she's really upset but she's just playin' yer, you get me?'

'No she ain't,' I told him.

Dean shrugged.

'I dunno why you and her don't just get together, man. It's obvious that you like her . . .'

I looked over at Grace, who was standing chatting to Hannah. Then I turned back to Dean.

'No I don't,' I told him, which was a lie. I did like her but I wasn't sure that she liked me and I didn't want to mess up nothing by asking her. Besides, she wouldn't want me anyway.

'What*ever*,' replied Dean, in a high pitched voice, pretending to be a girl. 'Don't be coming cryin' to me when it all hits the fan, girlfriend . . .'

I looked around us, embarrassed, but no one was listening. 'You're a weirdo, bro,' I told him.

Dean grinned. 'Look who's talking,' he said.

After school I had to go home. I asked Grace what she was doing but she had a birthday dinner to go to, for her cousin. I thought about going round to Dean's to play on his Playstation or calling for Hannah but they were both busy too. I let myself in and walked into the living room, which was still a complete mess, and wondered whether my mum was in. I called for her but the house was empty so I sat down on the sofa and turned on the TV, hoping that she'd gone for the night. But I couldn't relax. Everywhere I looked there were empty beer cans and ashtrays and stuff. And the place stank. I got up and went into the kitchen, shaking my head at the pile of dishes in and around the sink, grabbed a bin bag and went back into the living room. It took me nearly two hours to clear up everything, including the dishes, and when I was done I was so tired that I fell asleep on the sofa.

It was gone ten when I woke up. My stomach was rumbling and my head hurt. I looked around and saw that my mum hadn't come home. There was no food in either so I decided to go down to the chippie for the third time that week. I had homework to do for the next day but I decided that it could wait. I was hungry.

THREE

The next morning I got up early and had a shower. Then I looked around for some clean clothes but my mum hadn't done any washing. I knocked on her bedroom door, waiting to hear her mumble like normal, but this time the door opened and Micky was standing there, his hair all over the place and sleep in his eyes.

'What do yer want, you little shit?' he hissed.

'Nothing from you . . .' I told him, turning and heading back to my room, where I put on the same clothes that I'd been wearing for the last few days. At least it was Friday. I would be able to wash my uniform over the weekend.

I walked downstairs and made myself some coffee, stepping over the mess that my mum and Micky had left when they'd come in the previous night. So much for tidying up, I thought to myself. As I looked around I saw Micky's jacket. I picked up a can of lager, shook it to make sure there was something in it, and poured it over the jacket. Then I sat and watched morning telly and wondered how I was going to handle the weekend. I didn't like being at home when Micky was there and I knew that my mum was off work all weekend, which meant that he would be around all day, both days. I swore at the thought, took my mug into the kitchen, washed it, grabbed my bag and left the house, nearly an hour before I needed to.

I walked to the main road, past the daily traffic jam, heading to Grace's. I was trying to stop myself from getting angry about Micky but it wasn't working. I couldn't believe that my mum had let him back into the house after everything he had done before. I was really angry with her and if I had known where my dad was, I would have gone to him. But he didn't want me either, and I was kind of stuck. So I just got angrier as I walked, and by the time I reached the row of shops behind Grace's house I was so wound up that I had to sit down on a wall and calm myself. I put my hand in my pocket and realised that I only had a couple of quid to my name.

'Shit!' I said out loud, as a couple of men walked by, wearing blue overalls.

'Easy kid,' said one of them, smiling. 'Can't be that bad . . .'

I shrugged and kicked my feet, wondering how I was going to pay for my bus fare and eat too. I'd just have to pretend to be full at lunchtime again, or pick at what Dean ate. It wouldn't be the first time.

Opposite me there was a shop front with a clock above it and I realised it was just after eight. I jumped off the wall and went to call for Grace, straightening my hair as much as I could and brushing down my clothes. Her dad answered the door.

'Hello Jit!' he said, with a huge smile.

'Hi Mr Parkhurst. Is Grace ready to catch the bus yet?'

Grace's dad shook his head.

'No – she's running late so I'm going to give her a lift. Come in – and please, call me Michael . . .'

'OK,' I replied, following him into their kitchen.

'I'm having a cup of coffee. Would you like one?' he asked me.

I looked over at the gleaming silver coffee machine that he had bought recently and then around the kitchen, which was so clean you could have eaten off the floor. I nodded.

'If there's time,' I said.

Grace's dad grinned again. 'There's always time where Grace is concerned. I think she's in the shower . . . come on, let me show you how the machine works . . .'

I nodded. Mr Parkhurst had already shown me how it worked loads of times but he was kind of forgetful and I liked him so I didn't mention it. Grace appeared about ten minutes later.

'Hey Jit! When did you get here . . .?' she asked, looking surprised.

I thought that she might think I was mad or something so I coughed and looked away.

'Got the time wrong,' I told her. 'So I was a bit early . . .'

'Never mind!' boomed her dad. 'It meant that we got to spend some time together, Jit and I . . .'

Grace grinned. 'So now you're crawling to my dad?' she asked.

'Er . . .' I began, embarrassed that she thought that.

'*Well* . . . ?' she asked.

'No I ain't,' I finished. 'I was just early, that's all . . .'

She smiled at me and came and sat down.

'It's fine, you silly monkey bum,' she said, touching my arm.

I felt a shiver run across my chest and I pulled my arm away. What if she could smell my clothes, I thought. She'd think that I was a tramp. I stood up and tried to change the subject.

'Come on,' I told her, 'we've got to get to school.'

Grace looked at me like I was mad.

'Blimey, *what's up with you* . . . are you ill or something?'

'No!' I said quickly.

I didn't want her to know what was up with me. I

didn't want anyone to know. Dean had found out a bit, a few weeks earlier, but that was a one-off. I could handle my own problems. I didn't want to stress my mates with them too.

'God – I was only *asking* . . .' she said, looking all upset.

'Er . . . I didn't mean . . . I er . . . come on,' I mumbled, like an idiot.

'OK people,' said Mr Parkhurst, rescuing me from foot in mouth. 'Time for school.'

I was in a good mood by the time we arrived at school. Mr Parkhurst had invited me over on Saturday night, along with everyone else, because we hadn't been over for dinner for a while. I agreed straight away, jumping at the chance to get away from my mum and Micky. Grace was happy about it too.

'We can work on the latest issue of the school newspaper,' she said, smiling.

'Is the next one coming up already?' I asked.

The newspaper had started a few months earlier, after our little gang had got into trouble over a scam to do with lunchtime social clubs, all of it caused by Dean. We had to put one together every month and it was OK really.

'*Yeah*,' replied Grace. 'Lots to do, monkey boy . . .'

I nodded and we got out of her dad's car and walked into school, ten minutes early. I hadn't been on time for ages and as I walked past Mr Singh, my football coach and year head, I was hoping for him to notice. He did, but not in the way that I wanted him to.

'You need to see me straight after registration,' he said to me.

'What?'

'My office, Jit. And if you can't work out why, you've got the next twenty minutes to do just that . . .'

I shrugged and turned to Grace.

'Dunno what's up with that knob,' I said.

Grace just shook her head. 'Maybe it's the lesson that you missed yesterday?' she reminded me.

'Er . . . yeah, *maybe*,' I replied.

I didn't say anything else as we walked to our form room. Instead, I was trying to think up a reason for skiving. Something that wouldn't make Mr Singh angry, or lead to a letter for my mum. Not that she'd read it anyway. She'd just get angry and tell me that I was waste of space. As we walked in, Mrs Dooher was handing out forms for parents to sign, giving permission for us to have our pictures taken. There was a Book Week coming up and we had a couple of authors coming into school. She handed me mine and then told me that I had to see Mr Singh.

'I know, Miss, I told her.

'Are you OK Jit?' she asked.

I shrugged. 'S'pose,' I said.

She told me to wait until everyone had gone.

'I just want a quick word with you. Nothing heavy . . .'

'Cool.' I smiled at her, before turning to Dean and the others. 'Easy . . .'

'Yes, bro,' replied Dean.

'You in trouble again?' asked Imi.

'Dunno,' I said.

'You need to stop skiving,' added Hannah. 'We don't want you to get kicked out or nothing . . .'

I gulped down a load of air. I'd never even thought that I'd get into that kind of trouble – enough to get excluded. I started to get really worried.

'*Jit's not gonna get thrown out!*' yelled Grace, jumping in.

'OK, OK, Sister Gee!' grinned Dean. 'Ain't no one throwin' yer bwoifriend out of school . . .'

I gave Dean a dirty look.

'I *ain't* her boyfriend,' I told him.

I heard Hannah mumble something under her breath.

'*You what?*' I asked her.

She grinned at me. 'Oh – nothing,' she replied. 'Just talking to myself . . .'

'I ain't surprised,' Dean told us. 'No one else talks to her . . . on account of how mad she is . . .'

'You do talk a lot of nonsense, Hann,' Suky told her.

'Least I don't hide under the stairs to kiss my boyfriend,' countered Hannah.

'*I don't*!' replied Suky.

'Yeah, you do,' answered Dean. 'We all seen yer the other day . . . kissin' each other like you was lickin' food off a plate . . .'

'*URRGH*!' said Grace.

'Get lost . . .' replied Suky, looking at Imi.

'*Yeah* – get lost,' he said, repeating what Suky had said.

'*Oooh* – check out the *couple*!' laughed Hannah. 'They even say the same things . . . must be love!'

'As long as you don't start wearing her underwear, bro,' Dean said to Imi. 'Them kind of kinkiness can *gwaan* . . .'

They all burst into laughter, even Imi and Suky. I didn't. I just sat there and watched them, still thinking about what Mr Singh was going to say.

FOUR

First I had to get past Mrs Dooher. I waited around until everyone had left and then I got up and walked over to her desk.

'What did you want to see me about, Miss?' I asked her.

'Go and close the door first,' she told me.

When I returned to the table she looked up at me and tried to smile but her face looked disappointed instead. I started to feel angry with myself for being a knob.

'You know what I'm going to say, don't you?' she asked.

I shrugged.

'You can't just skip lessons whenever you like, Jit. It's not going to be tolerated . . .'

'Yeah, I know and I'm sorry but I wasn't feeling well and . . .' I started.

Mrs Dooher just shook her head slowly.

'There's always *something*, Jit. There's always an excuse. But now the other teachers are beginning to realise and, regardless of what you might think, we *do* talk to each other. Maths yesterday was the fourth lesson you've skipped in three weeks, only to turn up later in the day as though we wouldn't notice . . .'

I didn't know what to say so I nodded.

'Mr Singh isn't angry with you, he's worried. And so am I. We need to find out why you do it . . .'

'It's nothing really . . . I was just . . . I won't do it again,' I told her.

'That's just it, Jit. We spoke to your primary school and you were doing the same thing there too . . . what is it that makes you skip school . . . ?'

I looked away and I could smell my uniform, which made me even more determined not to say anything.

'What's up, Jit?'

'Nuttin',' I replied.

'Come on . . .' she said in her soft Liverpool accent. 'I wasn't born yesterday . . . I'm here to talk to if you need.'

'But . . .'

It went on like that for another few minutes and then I went off to see Mr Singh who repeated what Mrs Dooher had said for about half an hour.

Then he looked out of the window of his office. 'I'm going to have to take action,' he said, not looking at me.

'But I said I wouldn't do it again . . .' I protested.

'That's not enough, son. It can't be one rule for you . . . There are procedures we have to take as a school . . .'

'What – so you're just gonna hang me out to dry like

everyone else?' I spat out, instantly wishing that I hadn't said anything.

'Who's hung you out to dry?' he asked, looking at me this time.

'No one . . .' I mumbled.

'Jit?'

'No one, man. Just leave it . . . Ain't like you people care anyways. It's just summat you have to do – that's what you just said, weren't it?'

'No, that's not what I said at all. Why do you think that I'm sitting here talking to you?'

I looked at him, shrugged and looked away. 'I dunno . . . maybe 'cause you have to . . .'

Mr Singh shook his head. 'I'm here because I care about you. I've seen the way you walk from one bit of trouble to another . . . I know that something's wrong. All I'm trying to do is help you . . .'

'So, what you gonna do?' I asked him.

'Well that depends on you, Jit. The first thing is that I have to write a letter to your mum to tell her what's been going on . . .'

I wanted to groan but I didn't. My mum never read any letters from school.

'And then maybe we'll get her in and have a chat about things . . .'

'You can't do that!' I blurted. 'I don't want her to come

here . . . she's too busy anyways, always at work and that.'

'We can work around that, Jit,' he told me.

He took an envelope that was on his desk and gave it to me.

'That's for your mum. She needs to read it and get in touch with the school. She can call me any time she likes. I do need to talk to her before next Friday however . . . or I'll have to get her to come in . . .'

I didn't listen to what else he was saying. I was wondering how I was going to get out of the mess I was in. My mum wouldn't call the school and even if she would, I didn't want to give her the letter anyway. She'd just get angry and so would Micky and then he'd make my life even worse and my mum would end up drinking more. I didn't want that. I had to find a way to blag it only I couldn't work out what that would be.

'Are you listening to me, son?' I heard Singh say.

'Huh?'

He shook his head. 'I was saying that you need to attend your lessons from now on. This is your first real warning, Jit, and you won't get too many more . . .'

'Yessir,' I replied.

'Right, now sit here until break and then go and join your friends . . .'

'Thank you, sir,' I said.

'Oh and one more thing, Jit,' he said as he stood up

and grabbed his mug of coffee, 'if you *are* suspended you won't be eligible for the football team . . .'

I looked at him in shock. Football was one of the few reasons that I liked school at all. I couldn't get kicked out of the team. I nodded and told him that I understood.

The rest of the day went by in a haze. I tried to get into what my friends were doing but all I could think about was Singh's warning. It felt like I had the flu – you know, when you can't think clearly and your head feels like it's weighed down with something. It was even worse in our last lesson because I was so hungry. I felt weak and couldn't wait for the day to finish. When it did I told Grace and Dean that I'd see them the next day and I went home on my own, praying that Micky would be out. But as I opened the front door, I could smell cigarettes and I knew that my prayers hadn't been answered. I walked through to the living room and saw him lying on the sofa, watching some talk show. There were cans of cider on the floor beside the sofa and an overflowing ashtray. The curtains were drawn too and the room was all gloomy.

Not wanting to talk to him, I decided to go straight up to my room but it didn't work.

'You got any money?' he asked me.

'What?'

'Money . . . you deaf or summat?'

I turned to walk up the stairs.

'I'm talkin' to yer, you likkle dick . . .'

'Get lost . . .' I told him.

He jumped up from the sofa and stood over me, trying to look threatening. I looked into his face. I wanted to puke at the smell of his breath. He hadn't shaved and his hair was all lank and greasy.

'You tellin' me to get lost?' he sneered.

'So?' I asked, not wanting him to think that I was scared of him.

'You little . . .'

'You touch me and I'll stab you in the head . . .' I told him calmly.

'Just give me yer money or I'll throw you out again . . .' he threatened.

I backed down a bit and looked past him, wishing that my mum had been in to see the way he spoke to me. 'I ain't got no money,' I said. 'And even if I did . . . I wouldn't give you none . . .'

He sneered at me for a few seconds and then his eyes went dead and he grabbed the front of my jacket, swearing his head off. He dragged me to the door before I could do anything, opened it and threw me out into the street, slamming the door shut behind me. I stood and looked at the door as tears started welling in my eyes.

I tried really hard not to cry but I couldn't help it and then I got angry with myself for being so weak and I started kicking the door, over and over again, until I'd hurt my foot. But he didn't open it, and when I tried my key, which I still had, it wouldn't work because he had double locked the door from inside.

I stood for a while longer and then remembered that my mum was working until ten o'clock. I put my hand in my pocket and found fifty-four pence. Enough to get a packet of crisps. I kicked the door once more and swore at the top of my voice, so loud that my next-door neighbours looked out of their front window. Not that I cared. I did up my jacket, turned towards the main road and set off, not knowing where I was going to go, or what I was going to do until my mum got back.

FIVE

I walked down the main road towards the shops, watching all the people walking about and the traffic. There were loads of Muslim people around because it was Friday, their main prayer day, and as I walked past the mosque I watched the people standing around chatting, whilst the kids messed about in the car park, running around and stuff. I turned left and headed down a side street, just because I didn't have anything to do. The street was narrow, with cars parked both sides and ahead of me two Punjabi men were arguing over a parking space outside a greengrocer's. They were swearing at each other and some of the stuff they were saying was well nasty. As I went by they stopped for a few seconds, before one of them, who was wearing a turban, said something about the other one's mum. I left them to it though.

Further on I bumped into a couple of lads from school, Dilip and Paresh. They were kicking a ball across the road at each other, in between parked cars.

'Easy Jit!' Dilip said as I walked up.

'Easy . . .' I replied. 'What a gwaan?'

'Jus' chillin',' he told me. 'Too wet to go up the park and that so we's just kickin' about out here . . .'

'You better make sure you don't hit no car,' I said, with a grin. 'I seen the flat foot way you kick the ball at footie . . .'

Dilip grinned back. 'Kiss my ass, man . . .' he replied, as Paresh crossed the road to join us.

'What you doin' walking the streets anyhow?' asked Dilip.

I shrugged and told about half of the truth. 'Locked out – got time to kill . . . me mum ain't home until half-ten . . .'

Paresh shook his head. 'That's wack . . . so what you gonna do?'

I shrugged again. 'Whatever, you get me . . . Might go check on my boy Dean . . .'

'What . . . MC Rhymes Too Lame?' laughed Dilip.

'The self-same bwoi . . .' I told them.

Dilip looked at his watch and then told me he had to go in. I nodded and walked on, wondering if Dean or Hannah were around.

By the time I walked past the church down on St Philips Road for the fourth time, it was nine-thirty and I had been walking around in circles for hours. I turned back on myself and headed up the road, back towards my area. I walked by two chippies, a burger place, three pizza and kebab places and a Caribbean takeaway, getting hungrier each time. My head was light and it felt like there was nothing in my legs at all. And then I saw my mum heading out of an off-licence. She was in her uniform, wearing a coat over the top of it, and in her hand she had a bag full of booze.

'MUM!' I shouted.

She turned round, saw me and smiled.

'Hey baby . . .' she said, embarrassingly.

I walked up to her and she gave me a big hug.

'My baby . . .' she said about ten times.

I looked at her, realised that she was already drunk, and then hugged her some more.

'Micky didn't let me in . . .' I told her.

'Huh,' she asked, not really listening.

'Well I let myself in but he was mean to me and then he threw me . . .' I began, only to realise that my mum just wasn't paying any attention at all.

I sighed and let it go. 'You eaten yet, Mum?' I asked.

She shook her head.

'And how come you finished work early . . . ?' I asked.

'Dunno . . . who cares anyhow?' she said, smiling. 'You want chips, baby?'

I sighed again and nodded. Four times this week, I thought to myself. Not that I was bothered. I would have eaten a barbecued rat. We walked down the road, towards another chip shop and got some food before heading home. I wondered what Micky would say when he saw me with Mum but I knew that it wouldn't be a problem. There was no way he was going to bully me with Mum around. He was stupid but not *that* stupid. In the end he was sly about it.

'I must have fallen asleep,' he told my mum, as he opened the door. 'I think I double locked it by mistake . . .'

He gave me a look that told me to keep quiet.

'I'm ever so *sorry*, Jit . . .'

My mum wasn't listening though. She had opened a bottle of wine and was in the kitchen getting plates for our food. I looked at Micky and smiled. '*Not a word . . .*' he warned.

'You know – one of these days I'm gonna *get* you,' I warned back. 'You'll be out cold or have your back turned and I'm gonna do yer . . .'

'*You effing likkle . . .*!' he began, just as my mum walked in from the kitchen.

'You what . . . ?' she asked him, and for a second I hoped that she'd heard him. But she hadn't.

Micky turned on the cheese.

'I was just saying how much I *enjoy* being here with Jit . . . it's like we're *best* mates. Ain't that right, Jit?'

I looked at my mum, back at Micky and pretended to agree.

'Yeah . . . that's right, Mum.'

She smiled, as I sat down to eat my fish and chips. 'That's so lovely,' she replied. 'No, *really* . . .'

It was midnight when I got my dirty clothes together and put them in the washing machine. My mum and Micky had gone to sleep, leaving the living room in a stinking mess. I turned on the machine and tidied up the house, as I waited for the cycle to finish, so that I could put the clothes straight into the dryer. As I waited I watched late night telly, getting bored really quickly until I saw a programme about the latest computer games. I sat and watched that for a bit and then some lame film in German, before sorting out my clothes and heading for my bedroom.

As I walked past my mum's room, the door opened and Micky walked out. He smiled at me, grabbed me by the neck and held me against the wall.

'You think you're clever?' he whispered.

I didn't reply. Instead I stared at him, not letting him see that I was in pain. But my eyes were watering again.

'Next time you try and take me for a fool, I'll get really angry . . . and you ain't seen nothing like that, son . . . I promise.'

He let me go and went to the bathroom. I rubbed my neck, went into my bedroom and locked the door. I was tired but I was also angry and wound-up so instead of sleeping, I sat up for a few hours and tried to think of a way to get rid of Micky once and for all. It took me ages but in the end I had a brainwave. I actually fell asleep with a smile on my face . . .

I didn't wake up until eleven and when I went downstairs all of my clean clothes had been folded neatly. There was also an envelope on the table with my name on it, written in Mum's handwriting. I opened it. Inside was a twenty-pound note, and a letter. Mum and Micky had gone away, it told me, and wouldn't be back until the following day. The money was for food and there was big kiss at the foot of the letter. I sat down, relieved that I wouldn't have to deal with Micky, and thought about how much I didn't want him to be in Mum's life. She was different around him, always smoking and drinking, and I was worried that it was going to make her ill. As I sat and thought about it, I became even more determined to get rid of Micky. My plan was going to take a bit of work, maybe even a bit of help from my mates. Even if I had to let them know how bad things really were, I didn't mind. The shame would be worth it if I could get rid of the grease ball.

SIX

I was the first one to get to Grace's house, followed five minutes later by Hannah and Dean. I was in her cellar, setting up a game of pool when they walked in. Dean gave me a funny look.

'Man, we just called for you and you is already here . . .' he said.

'Yeah – we knocked for ages and no one answered,' said Hannah.

I shrugged. 'You didn't tell me that you were gonna call for me,' I replied.

'Yeah but we never do,' said Hannah. 'Your mum out or something?'

I nodded. 'Yeah – she's gone away with—'

'She got a new man?' asked Hannah.

I was about to tell her the truth but something in my head stopped me and I told her a lie instead.

'Nah . . . she's with an aunt . . .'

'Oh, right . . .'

Dean took the cue from my hands and broke off a new game. 'Enough chit chat – time to get beat at pool by the Number One . . .' he announced.

Grace looked at Hannah and smirked. 'More like a Number Two,' she said giggling.

Dean shook his head. 'See how you go on, Sister Gee? And I'm so nice to you too, man . . .'

Grace grinned.

'I'm soooo sorry, Deany-Beany-Boy. I didn't mean to upset you,' she teased.

'Yeah – don't have tantrum,' said Hannah.

'Just watch the master at work,' Dean replied.

Hannah looked at Grace. 'He used to throw tantrums at junior school. Like if he was tryin' to talk to you and you didn't listen – he used to cry like a baby . . .'

'No! I don't believe you,' replied Grace. 'Not big bad Dean . . .'

'You two are bad,' I told them.

'Don't bother me, bro,' said Dean. 'Least I grew up. Hannah still goes on like a baby and as for Grace . . .'

'Grace ain't a baby,' I told him.

'You tell him, Jit!' said Grace, smiling at me.

Dean handed me the cue and shook his head slowly. 'You're supposed to back me up,' he told me. 'You'll be wearing skirts next, bro . . .'

'Oh shut up, you dick,' said Hannah. 'Don't listen to him Jit – he's just stupid . . .'

'Least I ain't got a fat ass,' said Dean, winking at me.

Hannah grabbed the cue out of my hands and pointed it at Dean.

'I'm gonna shove this cue right up your fat ass . . .'

'I do wish you'd get over this fixation with Dean's bottom,' said Mr Parkhurst, appearing at the foot of the stairs.

Everyone laughed except Hannah, who went bright red. Grace's dad was always catching her out just as she was threatening Dean. It happened so often that it was getting silly.

'I'm sure that there are therapists who can help,' continued Mr Parkhurst.

'I was only—' began Hannah, going red again.

'Oh Dad – stop teasing her,' Grace told him.

Mr Parkhurst looked at me and Dean and winked.

'Looks like I've been told,' he said. 'Now who wants to help me sort out dinner?'

I shrugged and looked at Dean who shook his head.

'I got this disease, Mr Parkhurst,' he replied. 'Summat 'bout how I can't do no housework 'cause it might kill me . . . Nohelpyitis or something.'

Grace's dad laughed.

'Sounds nasty,' he said. 'Is it contagious . . . like those spots you seem to get regularly . . .'

'NAH!!!!!!!!!!!!!!!' I shouted. 'Dissed by the old man . . .'

'DAD!' shouted Grace, trying not to laugh too much.

Dean shook his head, picked up another cue and went back to playing pool.

'What are we having for dinner?' asked Hannah.

'Sausage and mash,' beamed Grace's dad. 'Made by my own hand . . .'

'But Hannah and I are vegetarians,' protested Grace.

'Yes, I know that,' replied her dad. 'That's what the veggie sausages are for . . .'

'Oh, right,' said Grace. 'I like those . . .'

Hannah looked at Grace. 'Are they nice?' she asked.

'Mmmm!' Grace replied like a little girl.

Dean snorted. 'Surely you shouldn't eat sausages if you're vegetarian . . .' he said.

'But they're made of soya and stuff,' said Grace. 'There's no meat in them, stinky boy.'

'Yeah – I know that,' said Dean. 'But sausages are normally meat, right? So if you were a grass eater – why would you want sausages? I mean – you don't get vegetarian steak and kidney, do yer?'

Grace looked at him like he was mad. 'But that's what we just said . . . that's why they're vegetarian . . .'

Dean shook his head. 'I just reckon you're desperate to eat meat, only you'll look silly because you're always goin' on about animals and that . . .'

'God! Sometimes you're so . . .' began Hannah.

'So, instead you eat vegetarian sausages and pretend

that they're really made of pork or beef or . . .'

'OK!' shouted Grace's dad, grinning even wider. 'Let's just get them cooked shall we? You can have a debate about them afterwards.'

I looked at Mr Parkhurst and smiled. 'Would you like me to help you?' I asked.

'*Would you like me to help you,*' mimicked Hannah.

'Yeah – can I be *captain licky bum*, sir?' added Grace.

Dean shook his head again and looked at me.

'Witches,' he said. 'You get me?'

By the time that Imtiaz and Suky turned up, together, the food was ready. Mr Parkhurst had piled a load of sausages onto two separate plates, one for meat and the other for non-meat. I helped him take everything through to their dining room, which was almost the same size as the whole ground floor of my mum's house. The gang were sitting round the table, waiting, and Dean was teasing Suky. Grace's dad asked him why.

'They's bumping uglies . . .' Dean told him.

'I'm sorry?' asked Mr Parkhurst, looking confused.

'Dean means that Imi and Suky are going out with each other,' explained Hannah.

Mr Parkhurst smiled. 'Excellent!' he said. 'I always knew there'd be couple amongst you . . . too much bickering for there not to be,' he said.

I didn't have a clue about what he meant but I nodded anyway and smiled. Imi tried to change the subject.

'Where's your mum, Grace?'

'She's away for the weekend with work,' replied Grace.

'Don't change the subject, Lover Bwoi!' shouted Dean.

'Oh shut up!' Suky told him. 'You're such a little boy sometimes . . .'

'Man,' corrected Dean. 'Ain't no boy sitting here . . .'

'You looked in the mirror lately?' replied Suky.

'Yeah – unlike you . . . did you even brush your hair this morning?' countered Dean.

Suky gave him a death stare.

'Enough . . .' said Grace's dad. 'Let's eat before my mountain of mashed potato goes cold . . .'

He told everyone to help themselves and went to get some gravy.

'Fool!' whispered Suky to Dean.

'Tramp . . .' replied Dean.

'Just eat your food, will you.' Grace told them. 'You can have a fight afterwards . . .'

Dean shrugged.

'We need to talk to you all later anyway,' said Imi, looking at Suky.

''Bout what?' mumbled Dean, spitting food everywhere.

'URGH!! Dean!' shouted Suky.

'Sorry,' he said, after he'd swallowed what was left.

'Dutty, nasty little bwoi . . .' said Hannah.

Dean shoved half a sausage into his mouth and chewed it really fast.

'So, what you need?' I asked.

'Just . . . well . . .'

'Lessons in Lurrve?' asked Dean, spitting more food out.

'DEAN!' shouted Grace.

'Sorry, Sister Gee,' he said, not meaning it.

'We'll tell you in a bit,' said Suky, looking at me.

I expected her to look away but she didn't. Instead she kept her eyes on mine for another few moments and in the end it was me who looked away.

'This food's great Mr Parkhurst,' said Hannah, as he returned from the kitchen.

He sat down and piled a load onto his plate. 'Call me Michael, please,' he said.

I saw Dean grin and knew exactly what was coming.

'How ya' doin', Michael Please?'

Grace's dad looked at me, picked up a vegetarian sausage and threw it at Dean, who ducked. The sausage flew past his head and landed on a side table, next to a pair of glasses and a lamp. We all looked at each other in shock and then we pissed ourselves laughing.

SEVEN

Later on, while Hannah and Dean argued over another game of pool, Suky and Imtiaz told me what they wanted. Grace was sitting right next to me and I could feel her thigh against mine. I could even smell the shampoo she had used on her hair. It felt kind of nice to be so close to her but then I began to wonder if my clothes smelt and I got all embarrassed and moved my leg.

'You OK . . . ?' asked Grace, looking worried.

'Er . . . yeah – 'course I am. Why wouldn't I be?'

'Just wondered,' she told me, as Suky sat down on my other side.

'Wondered what?' she asked.

'I was wondering what's up with Jit,' Grace told her. 'He keeps trying to get away from me – I'm beginning to think that I smell . . .'

Not wanting her to think that, I told her that she smelt nice.

'*AHH*!' Suky said, taking the piss.

'So what did you want?' I asked her, changing the subject.

'Oh right . . . *that*,' she replied.

Imi came and sat down opposite us, as behind him, Hannah called Dean a rat. Suky looked at Imi and then back at me.

'My mum and dad want to meet Imi,' she said.

'That's lovely!' answered Grace, looking really excited.

'Not exactly,' Imi told us.

I looked at him and knew what was up straight away.

'It's that Sikh-Muslim thing innit?' I said to him.

He nodded.

'But what's that got to do with the price of boiled tuna?' asked Grace.

'You what?' replied Suky, looking confused.

'Boiled tuna,' repeated Grace. 'Price of . . .'

Suky looked at her like she was mad. 'Yeah . . . right . . . er . . . *anyway* . . .' she began.

'Suky ain't told her parents that I'm Muslim,' Imi admitted.

I shook my head.

'Yeah but how many Sikh lads are called Imtiaz?' I asked. 'They prob'ly worked it out from yer name, bro . . .'

Imi looked straight at Suky instead of answering. She started to go red.

'I . . . er . . . well, I haven't told them Imi's name,' she admitted.

Grace screwed up her nose. 'So what do they think he's called?' she asked. 'Do you just call him the boyfriend?'

'Er . . .' began Suky, only for Imi to take over.

'That's why we need *you* to do us a favour,' he said to me.

'Yeah, and what's that exactly?' I asked, getting suspicious.

Suky jumped in. 'OK – we may as well tell you. I'm worried that my dad won't like me going out with a Muslim boy so I told them that I was seeing a Sikh lad . . .'

'Called Imtiaz?' asked Grace.

Suky shook her head.

'No – a boy, called Jit . . .'

For a split second what she said didn't kick in but then it hit me.

'YOU WHAT?' I half shouted.

'Er . . . sorry,' replied Suky, looking embarrassed.

'Yeah . . . sorry bro,' added Imtiaz.

I looked at Grace who started to grin.

'You told your dad that you were going out with Jit?' she asked.

'Er . . . yeah, I suppose I did,' replied Suky.

'*JIT*?' repeated Grace.

'Yeah – what's the big deal?' Suky asked, playing it cool.

'The thing is . . . Suky's parents are kind of chilled out about her havin' a boyfriend . . .' Imi told us.

'They thinks it's cute,' said Suky, looking shamed.

'So, anyway, they're having a get together next weekend and I'm . . . I mean you're . . .'

I nearly dropped the glass of juice I was holding.

'NAH . . . *no way*! I ain't . . .' I began, only Grace's laughter stopped me.

'It ain't funny, Grace,' I told her.

'WHAT AIN'T?' shouted Dean from behind us.

'Jit . . . goin' out with Suky,' Grace managed to get out.

'EH?' replied Hannah, looking confused. 'But I thought that Imi was going out with . . .'

Dean grinned at me. 'Yes my dan! You is one dark horse, blood—'

'But I ain't goin' out with her,' I protested. Well, I wasn't. And I wouldn't either.

'It's just one evening Jit,' said Suky. 'Please . . .'

I stood up and walked over to the pool table, leaning against it. They were all mad. All of them.

'What happens if they invite me over again?'

'We can cross that bridge when we get to it,' argued Imi.

I shook my head. 'I ain't crossing no bridges, ain't jumping off no cliffs and I ain't pretendin' to be you for Suky's dad . . .'

'And the rest of her family . . .' said Imi. 'There's a load of aunts and uncles coming . . .'

'Yeah, it's my brother's birthday party,' Suky added.

'It still ain't happening . . .' I told them.

Everyone was quiet by that point and they were all sitting down except for me. I waited for someone else to speak.

'Well I don't see what all the fuss is,' said Hannah. 'I mean – do you *know* that your dad won't like Imtiaz, Suky?'

Suky didn't say anything.

'*Well* . . . ?' I added.

'I just *know*, all right. It's that whole religion thing. I mean, even if my dad was chilled about it, and he's pretty cool – the rest of my family wouldn't be happy . . .'

Grace put her hand up like she was at school and Dean saw her.

'Yes, Miss Parkhurst – anything you'd like to say?' he asked, in a deep voice.

'Yes sir . . . I was wondering why it was anyone else's business,' said Grace.

Suky sighed.

'Look, it's not the same for you,' she told Grace. 'This is one of those Asian tradition things . . . I don't mean to be rude, Grace, but you just wouldn't understand, OK?'

'You're not being rude,' Grace told her. 'You're just assuming that your dad won't like Imi because he's Muslim – but what if you're *wrong*?'

Suky shook her head. 'I'm not . . .' she said.

I looked at Dean, who shrugged. Something didn't make sense to me and I said so.

'Why don't you just say that your boyfriend is away with his family . . .' I asked.

'Yeah – tell them *Jit* is in Birmingham or somewhere,' said Dean.

Imi shook his head this time.

'Used that one already,' he said.

'Yeah, about six times,' added Suky. 'My dad thinks that I've made him up.'

'But you have,' said Dean. 'You *have* made him up, Suky . . .'

'Well,' said Grace, grinning, 'I think that Jit *should* do it – it'll be *funny* . . .'

'For you lot maybe . . .' I said. 'I still ain't doin' it.'

'*Please* . . .' begged Suky. 'It'll be OK . . . honest. It's just one evening . . .'

'Why should I?' I asked them.

'As a favour to your friends?' suggested Hannah.

I glared at her. '*What* – you in on this too?'

Hannah shrugged. 'I don't see how one evening is gonna make a difference . . .'

I sighed. 'What happens when they wanna see her boyfriend again?'

'Oh *yeah* . . .' agreed Dean.

'*See*? Finally one of you is getting me . . .'

'Or *Imi* could go as Jit . . .?' suggested Grace. 'How are your family gonna know he isn't *called* Jit?'

Suky shook her head.

'They know him from school events,' she told us. 'They've met him loads of times . . .'

'We've been through every option,' said Imi, 'and this is the *only* one.'

I stood where I was and shook my head over and over again.

'I ain't doing it,' I told them.

EIGHT

The next day I woke up early and decided to make the most of having the house to myself. I went round and tidied up really quickly, had a shower and found some clean clothes. Then I went into the kitchen to see if there was anything to eat. I found a few eggs, some bread and a bit of bacon so I cooked those and had them with some tea. It was really good not to have Mum and Micky around, complaining about hangovers or telling me to shut up all the time.

Then I went for a walk and bought a newspaper. I'd found some money whilst tidying up. It had been stuck down the back of the sofa and probably belonged to Micky, which made spending it seem even more fun. I walked home and read the sports section, wondering when my stupid footie team would get better. I had the TV on nice and loud, and just for the hell of it, I put Mum's little stereo on too, although her taste in music is lame. It was all to show that I was the boss, although there wasn't anyone around to see it.

But I didn't care. Just being relaxed was enough for

me, not wondering all the time about what kind of mood Micky was in. Or worrying about how drunk my mum was. Almost like normal.

But I still got bored and around two in the afternoon I decided to go and call Grace. I picked up the phone to call her only to find that the line was dead. It wasn't the first time. Micky had probably spent the money on booze or some greyhound at the bookies. My mum was always having to pay for the line to be reconnected. Instead I decided to go round to Hannah's first and try and call Grace from there.

Hannah was half asleep when she answered the door and gave me a funny look when I asked if I could use the phone. Her robe was falling open and I could see her bra, which was pink. I looked away, then back again, and then away once more.

'What's up with yours?' she yawned at me.

'Knackered . . . go on – it's only to call Grace . . .' I said.

Hannah nodded and led me into the house. There was just one room that led through to the kitchen, just like my mum's, only Hannah's was clean and smelled of flowers not fag smoke and spilled booze. She pointed at the phone before she spoke.

'OK, but be quiet – Mum's asleep . . .'

'She been on nights?' I asked, wondering if I should

tell Hannah that she was flashing me. But I didn't.

'Yeah . . . your mum too?'

I shook my head. 'Nah she's gone away for the weekend . . . see her brother,' I told her.

Hannah raised an eyebrow.

'You said her sister yesterday,' she replied.

'What?'

'Her sister . . . you said it was her sister . . .'

I looked away.

'Whatever . . . can I use the phone or not?' I snapped, regretting it straight away.

Hannah was my oldest friend. I'd known her for four days longer than I'd known Dean, and she was used to me being an idiot, I reckon. She didn't get upset, just smiled and told me I was a shithead.

'I might come with you,' she yawned.

'Cool . . . but you'd better get dressed . . . yer robe thing is half open,' I told her, trying not to look. Again.

She glanced down, said 'Oops!' and pulled it closed.

'Bet you copped a right eyeful,' she grinned at me.

'Weren't lookin',' I lied.

Hannah pulled a face. 'You're only interested in Grace – is that it?' she said, teasing me.

'*No*!' I said loudly.

'I think my lad doth protest too mucheth . . .' she said through another yawn.

'You *what*?'

'It's from some play or summat,' she told me.

'Just go get dressed, man and let me call Grace . . .'

'Ooh,' replied Hannah, in a French accent. 'Check out Meester Masterful . . . I think I like it, *Cherie* . . .'

We spent the afternoon playing pool and chatting about school, and every ten minutes or so Hannah and Grace asked me why I had been so funny about helping Suky and Imtiaz out. I kept changing the subject, not wanting to go over it again and again but they didn't let up.

'I just think it's stupid, that's all,' I told them.

'But it'll be a laugh,' Grace told me.

'For *you lot* maybe . . . What do I know about Suky's dad? What if he don't like me or he finds out the truth?'

Hannah shrugged.

'That's Suky's problem . . .' she said. 'But you could help her out. We are supposed to be friends, all of us.'

'Yeah and that's what friends do,' added Grace, 'help each other.'

'I still ain't doin' it,' I told them.

Grace shook her head. 'What if *you* need help one day?'

'I don't,' I said.

'Yeah but what if you did?' she repeated, only I wasn't really listening.

Instead I was trying to think of my plan to get rid of Micky, and about how I was an arse because I probably *would* need my friends to help me. I didn't let on to Hannah and Grace though. I wanted to think about Suky's idea a bit more first. I shrugged.

'OK then – let me have a think about it,' I told them.

'YEAH!!!' Grace grinned. 'You'll be the nicest, loveliest boy in the whole school if you help them . . .'

'Yeah – you'll get so much good karma you'll come back as a very rich man,' added Hannah.

I didn't have a clue what she was on about.

'Eh?'

'Karma . . . good energy. It's from Buddhism . . .' explained Hannah.

'Yeah – like reincarnation,' agreed Grace. 'If you're nice in this life you'll be reborn into a better one . . .'

'You know what – there's crackheads round my way that don't talk as much mad shit as you two . . .' I replied.

'*Ooh*! Wanna be careful – swearing – that's bad karma,' said Hannah.

'That's at least five thousand karma points lost,' added Grace. 'You've just dropped from a possible king to a rabbit . . .'

Hannah grinned. 'Even worse. I reckon you're gonna

come back as a politician . . . all cheesy and greasy and lyin' all the time.'

'A fate worse than *death*,' agreed Grace.

'*Much worse*,' added Hannah.

'Like the worst thing that you can think of – times a *billion*,' said Grace.

'*Worse City* . . . the streets where things can't get any . . .' began Hannah.

'*Worse*,' finished Grace.

I just sat where I was and shook my head at them. They were nuts.

Later on, when I got in, I realised that I was going to need all the help I could get. My mum and Micky were back and they were sitting on the sofa waiting for me when I walked in. My mum smiled at me and told me to sit down. Micky shifted along so that I could sit next to him but I stayed where I was.

'What?' I asked, when she told me she had something important to tell me.

'We're going to get married,' she said.

My stomach turned over and I felt a sweat breaking on my forehead.

'Well?' she asked.

I nodded because that was all I could manage to do. My head was spinning. Micky looked at me with his stupid grin and I could see it in his eyes – what was going through his mind. *I've got you now, you little shit. I win . . .*

I felt the urge to throw up and tried to force it back.

'But . . .' I heard myself saying.

'He's going to move back in with us, baby . . . you've been getting on so well together. It'll be like a fresh start. A new family – won't it, Micky?' my mum said.

Micky grinned even wider.

'I told yer mam how we've got an understandin' now, Jit. Ain't that right . . . you an' me – we're like bestest mates, in't we?' he told me.

I couldn't think, couldn't speak. Instead I mumbled that I wasn't feeling well and ran upstairs to my room, my head spinning round and round. He'd done it. Got his way, like the rat that he was, and now I was gonna be stuck with him. Like he was trying to prove it, Micky walked into my room without knocking.

'Get out . . .' I told him.

'Now, now, son – no need for that. I'm gonna be here all the time and we're gonna have to get on . . .' he sneered.

I told him to get lost but he walked over to my bed and grabbed me by my throat again. His face was red and his eyes were bloodshot. I could smell his breath too and if he hadn't have been trying to strangle me, I would have thrown up because it smelt so bad.

''Cause if we don't,' he spat in a whisper, 'I'm gonna have to teach you a few lessons . . . understand?'

NINE

'I'll do it,' I told Suky the following Wednesday, as we were sitting watching the rain falling outside during lunchtime.

'What?' she asked, looking surprised.

'Your thing – 'bout being yer boyfriend for yer family . . . I'll do it,' I explained.

I thought that she would thank me and say that I was a good friend or something but instead she jumped up and gave a me hug and a kiss, just as Grace came walking up to us.

'You're *sooo* lovely – I *lurvve* you!' she screamed.

I pushed her away and looked at Grace, feeling guilty. Then I started to get mad at myself for feeling that way and I had to count to ten, like Mr Singh had taught me in football, to calm myself down. When I'd finished I turned to Suky.

'There's no need to cover me in spit though, is there?' I said to her, smiling a bit.

'Am I interrupting something?' asked Grace, with a strange look on her face that I couldn't work out.

'No . . . I was just . . .' I began, only Suky grabbed me again.

'He was just saying how wonderful he is and how much he's gonna help me and Imi out!' she told Grace, before kissing me again.

'Gerroff!' I replied, pushing her away again.

Grace gave me another funny look and then sat down on a radiator. 'Well, that's nice,' she said.

'We'll have to get together before Saturday to go over a few things . . .' continued Suky.

'Like what?' Grace and me asked at the same time.

'Like *stuff*,' replied Suky, as if that made it clearer.

'What stuff?' I asked again.

'The things that a boyfriend is supposed to know . . . like what size feet I've got and my birthday and things,' she told me.

'But does Imi know what size feet you've got?' I asked her.

'That's not the point,' she replied. 'You've gotta know things about me – just in case my family ask you . . .'

'But why would they ask me?' I said, confused.

Suky grinned.

'You don't know my family . . . they're like proper secret agents. They'll ask you *loads* of stuff . . .'

I groaned. It was bad enough having to do it in the first place. I didn't want to have to sit through a test as well. I had school for that.

'And, besides . . .' said Suky, looking a bit shady, 'I've kind of told them what your dad does for a living . . .'

'But *I* don't know what my dad does,' I reminded her. 'I never see my—'

'So, *anyway*, I told them that he's a businessman – owns a load of shops. They liked that . . .' she butted in.

'That's a bit naughty,' said Grace.

'Naughty? That's just stupid . . . I don't look like someone whose dad is rich,' I complained.

'Oh, that don't matter,' said Suky, before realising what she'd done and going a bit red. 'I'm sorry – I never meant to . . .'

'S'OK,' I told her.

'So can we meet up somewhere – after school?'

I looked at Grace, not knowing why, and then back at Suky. I shrugged.

'S'pose,' I replied.

'OK then! We'll meet up after school and go and get a coffee or something . . .'

'And I can come too!' beamed Grace. 'It'll be fun . . .'

Suky shook her head. 'Why do you need to be there? Just me and Jit . . . Otherwise we'll just end up talking rubbish like we always do when we get together.'

Grace's face fell and she looked at me. I think I was supposed to say that she could come along too, but instead I just shrugged, like a knob head.

'*Fine*!' she said, all annoyed, before walking off.

'*Great*!' said Suky.

'What?'

'Well she's all *mardy-bum* now . . .'

I should have gone after Grace or said something but all I did was shrug. I was wondering when to mention that I needed a favour too. In the end I decided that I would speak to Dean first and see what happened after that. I told Suky I'd see her after school and went off to find Dean.

I found him talking to Wesley and Robert, trying to sell them a load of CDs. They were ignoring them and instead giving Dean the latest news on the Dark Lord.

'. . . We were checking the website just last night,' Robert was saying as I reached them. 'The two sequels are done. The author thinks that they are due to come out in time for Christmas.'

'Yes – which means that as well as getting myself the *Beginner's Guide to Hazelwitch* and the board game, I can also get two new stories . . .'

'Man, you're gonna have a fantasy filled Christmas . . .' laughed Dean, before turning to me. 'Whaddya think, Jit?'

I nodded.

'Yeah – great . . . though my idea of a fun Christmas wouldn't be reading books . . .' I said.

'Yeah an' wass all dat *Beginner's Guide* shite, bro?' Dean asked Wesley.

'Oh, that! It's exactly what it says – a guide to the magical world of Hazelwitch and all the characters,' replied Wesley.

'But you two know everything about it already,' I pointed out.

'Yeah – I bet you even know what Princess Wondlebarn's bra size is!' laughed Dean.

Wesley and Robert looked at each other in confusion. 'I'm not sure that it goes into *that* much detail,' said Robert.

'What? You don't get to see the Princess in her underwear . . . that's harsh, you get me?' I said.

'But . . . I'm not sure that I'd want to see . . .' began Robert.

'Yeah, but didn't you say that she looks like some fit woman off the telly?' asked Dean.

'In my head . . . yes,' admitted Robert.

'An' when you're lyin' in yer bed at home, feelin' all teenage and that – you tellin' me you don't picture her in her underwear or even less, bro?'

'Erm . . .'

''Cause dat would make you a liar, Roberto, and if yer lyin', well then yer flyin' . . .' finished Dean.

'I'm not . . . I wouldn't . . .' stammered Robert but I

started to feel sorry for him so I told Dean to leave it.

'He's only having a laugh with you,' I told Robert and Wesley.

Wesley nodded. 'We know,' he said. 'But it's a damn sight more interesting locking horns with you two than most of the others . . .' he said.

I didn't really get him but I nodded anyway – like I did in most of my Maths lessons, when in my head I was like Homer Simpson thinking about doughnuts or something, and not what was on the board.

'Yes . . . most of the other bull . . . I mean boys just beat us up,' added Robert, looking kind of sad.

'Yes,' agreed Wesley, 'you two are kind compared to them.'

I sensed that we were about to go down a road I didn't want to walk down so I told Wesley and Robert that we'd see them later.

'Come man – I wanna ask you summat,' I told Dean.

Dean watched Wesley and Robert walk away like he was a crocodile watching its prey.

'But I was about to mek some money . . .' he protested.

'Later, man. I need your help . . .' I told him.

That got his attention and he asked what was wrong.

'Some of them older lads bothering you?' he asked me.

I shook my head. The older bullies were the least of my worries. I had one of my own at home and I wanted rid of him. But I didn't know how to start telling Dean. It was him I'd had to go to when Micky had played up the first time. Dean's mum had let me stay and talked to my mum, who threw Micky out and promised me that he'd never come back. But somehow he'd wormed his way back in and now he was ten times worse than before. And I was too embarrassed to tell Dean about it. Only I didn't really have a choice any more and if any of my mates were gonna help me without even blinking, it would be Dean.

'I got a serious problem,' I told him.

His face clouded over and he sat down on the stairs that led up to English.

'What's up?' he asked.

'I need your help to . . . I gotta . . . I . . . Look I need your help to get rid of my mum's boyfriend . . .'

TEN

I explained what was going on with Micky to Dean and he got really angry. He wanted to talk to his mum again but I told him to forget about it.

'It'll just cause more grief and anyway your mum helped out last time and he still came back,' I told him.

'Yeah but surely your mum can see what's happening?' he said.

'She doesn't see a thing — that's what makes me so angry. It's like he's playing a game and he's good at it. It's all smiles when Mum's around and then when she's out of the way his real personality comes through.'

'I still can't believe she don't know . . .' he said, shaking his head.

I wondered whether I should tell him about her drink problem. I didn't want to but in the end I decided that I had to. It would make her reactions easier to understand.

'Er . . . my mum — she's got a problem,' I said.

'I'll say, bro,' agreed Dean.

'Nah – you don't get it. She's got a drink problem . . . they're always drunk when they're together . . .'

'Serious?' he asked.

'Yeah . . . I mean she goes work and that but—' A couple of girls from our class walked by so I lowered my voice. 'But she's definitely got a problem . . .'

Dean shook his head.

'I'm sorry, bro – I dunno what to say . . .' he told me.

'Just help me with my plan,' I replied. 'I can handle my mum – it's just that dick-head I need to get rid of.'

Dean looked puzzled. 'So how we gonna do that – kidnap him?' he asked.

I shook my head.

'Nah – nuttin' like that.'

And then I told him my plan.

Mr Singh caught me later on the same day, between the last two lessons. He asked me if I'd given my mum the letter.

'Er . . . yeah I have . . . she said she'd call you on Friday.'

I hadn't shown her the letter at all. It was still in my bag but I had to think of an excuse quickly so that Singh wouldn't get angry.

'She can't call until about three-ish – is that OK?' I said.

'Well it's a bit late but . . .' he began.

'She don't finish work until then so . . .'

'Doesn't, Jit. She doesn't finish work . . .'

I shrugged. 'That's what I said, weren't it?'

Mr Singh sighed and took a swig from the mug of coffee he was carrying.

'Never mind . . . just make sure that she does call and then come and see me before you leave school on Friday – do I make myself clear?' he said.

I nodded. But I didn't have any intention of hanging around on Friday afternoon. By the time he'd realised my mum wasn't going to call, I'd be long gone. That way I could deal with the problem the following Monday – once I'd helped Suky out and got the others to help with my plan too. Mr Singh and his letter could wait.

'Now get to your lesson and don't forget football practice is tomorrow after school,' he said.

'Yessir . . .' I replied, heading off for English.

When I got to the classroom Grace was waiting for me. We always sat at the same table and she was pretending to read something when I walked over.

'You all right?' I asked.

'Hmm?'

'Are you OK?' I repeated.

She looked up from her book and nodded.

'Why wouldn't I be?' she snapped.

I was going to say something but I didn't want to upset

her. I couldn't work out why she was angry either, so I shrugged.

'No reason,' I told her, sitting down.

She turned away from me and carried on reading. There was definitely something up with her. I looked at the book she was reading and laughed.

'It's upside down, Grace,' I told her.

'Isn't!' she said quickly.

'Grace . . . ! The book is the wrong way round.'

She turned the book around and smiled.

'I was just practicing my upside down reading,' she told me.

'Yeah – and why's that?' I asked, grinning.

'Why not – I might be trapped in a small, locked room one day, and the only instructions on getting out might be stuck to the ceiling. Only I won't be able to move, as I'm tied up, and I'll have to read it all upside down and . . .'

'Grace?'

'Hmm?'

'Will you just shut up and tell me what's wrong with you?' I said.

She closed the book and put it down.

'Nothing . . .' she said.

'Why don't you share your conversation with the rest of the class?' said Mr Herbert.

''Cause it's private, you knob,' I said quietly.

'WHAT DID YOU SAY, KOONER?' he shouted, going all red in the face.

'He called you a *knob*, sir,' squealed a lad called David.

I span round and glared at the grass.

'*Yeah*?' said David.

'I'm gonna *batter* you . . .' I told him, getting out of my chair.

David sat back, looking all worried. Then he started squealing again.

'*Sir*! *Sir*!'

Herbert told me to sit down about four times before he came over and stood in front of me.

'This is the last time I'm going to ask you . . .' he told me.

'*And then what*?' I asked him. 'You gonna use those skinny little arms to make me sit down?'

In my head Herbert's face changed into Micky's and I wanted to punch it but I stayed where I was.

'*RIGHT*! Get out . . .! Now,' shouted Herbert, his voice getting higher as he shouted.

My mind clicked back into the room and I saw Herbert's red face and the giant boil he had on the end of his nose. I started laughing and walked out of the room. In the corridor, Herbert told me that he wasn't going to tolerate my bad behaviour any more.

'I'm going to report you to Mr Singh . . .' he said.

'You wanna do that on Friday,' I told him, grinning.

'I'm sorry, young man?'

'Don't be,' I told him, noticing the other kids looking through the glass in the door, 'ain't your fault you were born ugly . . .'

I thought about how much trouble I was going to be in and then I told myself it didn't matter, and I walked off towards Mr Singh's office.

I got the usual grief from Mr Singh but then he asked me if everything was OK at home. I started wondering what he knew and how and then I just clammed up and said nothing. In the end he let me go and said that he was going to have to have a serious chat with my mum on Friday when she rang.

By the time I met Suky after school it was all I could think about and I didn't really pay her much attention.

'You're not listening,' she said, as we sat in a little café near her house.

'What?'

'*See*? Is something wrong, Jit?' she asked.

I shook my head. 'Nah – just the usual . . .'

Suky looked at me funny. 'How come you always get into trouble? I mean you aren't stupid but you always manage to upset the teachers . . .'

'It's my one skill,' I joked.

'*Jit* . . .'

'It's just Herbert – he's got it in for me,' I said, repeating what I had said to Mr Singh.

'That's rubbish . . .' she replied.

I looked out of the window.

'Just tell me what I need to know,' I told her.

'Man, sometimes you can be a right freak,' she said, before smiling.

She told me all about her family and warned me that her dad would ask me loads of questions about my family. The one that Suky had made up for me, that is.

'Oh and my grandmother is a bit senile,' she told me.

'*Great* . . .'

'And she might ask you loads of really weird stuff . . .'

'Like what?' I asked.

'Dunno . . . she just might so be prepared . . .' Suky replied.

'You want me to wear a *turban* an' all?' I joked. 'Pretend that I'm a good Sikh boy and that?'

She grinned at me.

'Idiot . . .'

I looked at her and smiled.

'There's summat I need from you too,' I told her.

'*What*?' she asked, raising her eyebrows.

'Just summat. I'll tell you all about it at the weekend . . .'

'Ooh, mystery boy . . . !' she said, laughing afterwards.

'You'll see,' I told her, secretly looking forward to our little arrangement. The more I thought about it, the more it seemed like it would be a laugh. Just what I needed.

ELEVEN

The rest of the week went by without anything happening and on the Friday afternoon I got out of school as soon as the final bell went, hoping that Mr Singh wouldn't see me. He didn't because he was too busy chatting up Miss Khan, another of our teachers, and I managed to get on the bus behind his back. All the way home I was worried that he might turn up at the house, asking to see my mum, but he would have had a job. She was working the night shift and when I got in she was just on her way out.

'Ain't you a bit early?' I asked, knowing that her shift didn't start until nine o'clock.

'Just gotta do some stuff, baby,' she replied, smiling.

She looked all tired and drawn and there were lines around her eyes. I wanted to tell her to stay at home, to take the night off. Not because I thought she was ill. I just didn't want to be on my own with Micky.

'I'm going to see a friend and then I'm getting a lift from Sarah,' she added.

'Oh . . .' Sarah was Hannah's mum.

'I've left you some stuff for dinner and Micky's got money if you want to get a kebab or something.'

'Cool,' I replied, realising that I was going to have to get my own food.

'You been OK?' she asked me, ruffling my hair.

'Mum . . .'

'Everything good at school . . . ?'

I shrugged. 'Usual . . .' I told her.

'OK . . . I'd better go. I'll see you tomorrow, baby . . .'

She kissed me on the cheek and I could smell the alcohol on her breath. Not much, but enough to know that she'd been drinking.

'Mum?' I began, thinking that I would say something about the booze, only I lost my bottle.

'Yeah . . . ?'

I shrugged again. 'Nuttin'. Have a good time at work.'

She grinned at me.

'Yeah, right. I'll sing like the dwarves in Snow White whilst I'm stacking canned carrots. You used to love that film when you were a baby . . .'

'I've grown up a bit since then,' I told her.

She gave me a hug, told me to be good and walked out of the door. I went into the living room and dumped my bag, before heading for my room. I came down just after six and went into the kitchen where Micky was on the phone to someone.

'Yeah . . . she's at work. Come roun' when yer like. Me casa is you casa an' all that foreign shite . . .' I heard him say.

He saw me and winked, putting the phone down.

'Awright?'

'When did the phone get put back on?' I asked him.

'Yesterday,' he replied.

'An' I suppose Mum paid for it – *again*?'

'None of yer business . . . we're getting *married* so we share everythin'. Just happens that she's workin' and I ain't . . .'

I gave him a dirty look and opened the fridge. He picked up a can of lager and cracked it open.

'I got a few mates comin' over tonight so don't get in me way,' he told me.

'*Can I at least get some food first?*' I snapped.

'Do what yer like but don't be askin' me for no money . . . I'm *skint*,' he said.

'But mum said she gave you some dough,' I told him.

He sneered at me. 'None of yer business that, my son. Now eat yer dinner and piss off out of it before I get angry . . .'

I was going to say something but decided against it. Instead, I rang Dean and asked him if I could stay over. He said that was cool and told me that he wanted to talk to me anyway. I rang off and made myself some fried eggs on toast, with two slices of old-looking bacon and a potato waffle. I ate in the kitchen too, standing up, and then washed the dishes, most of which weren't mine. Then I went up to my room and changed into my normal clothes. My uniform was dirty again but I didn't have time to wash it. I threw it on the floor and decided that I would sort it out in the morning.

Back downstairs, I pulled up the hood on my top, picked up the bag I'd put my change of clothes and toothbrush in, and told Micky where I was going.

'I don't care if yer goin' to the moon,' he replied, opening another can.

I swore at him under my breath and left the house.

Dean led me up to his room after I'd been round his entire family and said hello. They were eating when I got there and I had some food too, even though I'd eaten at home. His mum insisted and then his granddad told me that I was too skinny and needed to eat more.

'Look how yuh trousers hangin' off yuh raas, bwoi . . .' he said.

Dean jumped on his bed and told me to grab a chair. I sat at his desk, next to the turntables that we'd bought with the proceeds from a load of dodgy mobile phones.

'You wanna spin on them?' he asked.

I nodded. 'In a bit . . . can I play on that new game you got too?'

Dean grinned.

'*Me casa su casa . . .*' he said.

'Micky said that earlier . . . what's it mean?' I asked.

Dean shrugged.

'Like my house is your house or my gal is your gal or summat . . .'

'Ain't gonna be *gal*, is it?' I told him.

'True. I wouldn't share none of my gal wit' no one.'

I grinned. 'You ain't got a gal, you fool . . .'

Dean jumped off the bed and grabbed his mobile. It was the same as the last one I'd had only I'd sold mine because I needed the money.

'Is all *you* know, innit. Check out these digits, bwoi . . .'

I looked at the screen and saw the name Monica, a girl who was in the year above us.

'Don't mean it's her number,' I said, secretly jealous. Monica was fit.

'*Yeah, that's right, Dwight.* Like I'm really gonna just put her name and digits in deh for a blag . . .'

I looked at his face and saw the grin trying to break through.

'That's *exactly* what you done, innit?' I said, shaking my head. 'You ain't right in the brain, geezer, you get me?'

Dean pushed the dial button, holding his finger to his lips, telling me to keep quiet.

'*Yeah,*' he said, before lowering his voice, '*Er . . . YOW! Dat Monica? . . . Yeah it's D. Got my likkle virgin mate here don't believe this is your number . . . yeah dat skinny rass Asian brother . . .*'

Dean covered the mouthpiece, looked at me and mouthed the word 'shame'.

'What man – what's she sayin'?' I asked, getting pissed off.

Dean held his fingers to his lips again. '*. . . What . . . ? You wanna speak to him, yeah? You got a girl for him too . . . ? Yeah I think he'll go for that . . .*'

He held out the phone for me. 'Monica wanna talk to *you,*' he said.

I felt butterflies in my stomach and I tried to think of something to say but I couldn't. Dean grinned and thrust the phone into my hands. I put it to my ear.

'Er . . . hi . . . I mean . . . hello? Hello . . . ?'

Only there was no one on the other end.

'*MOVE WITH DAT*!!!!!!!!!!!!!' laughed Dean, falling down on his bed because he was laughing so much.

'You stupid—'

'Yuh get *blagged*, bro. *Big* time . . .' he grinned.

I shook my head but couldn't help smiling. He'd got me with a beauty and I knew it.

'I'm just gonna have to kick yer ass at that new game,' I told him.

'Forget that. You could beat me a *thousand* times but it ain't gonna kill the shame you feelin' . . . Yuh get scammed, blood. Well an' *proper* . . .'

I looked at his phone, flipped it shut and threw it at his head.

Later on, after I'd given him a kicking on his Playstation, we sat and chatted about my plan to get rid of Micky. I was determined it would work, and Dean wasn't so sure.

'How you gonna get him to do it?' he asked.

'Easy . . . I'm just gonna wind him up. He gets angry even when I don't. If I have a proper go at him, he'll snap . . .'

'Yeah but that's *dangerous*, man. What if he hurts you?' he added.

I shrugged.

'Don't care . . . as long as he falls for it. It's the only way Mum will go for it. She won't believe me no other way,' I told him.

'So why do you need *everyone* involved . . . ?'

'*Witnesses* . . .' I replied. 'The more, the better . . .'

'Man – I ain't too sure about this,' admitted Dean.

'It'll work . . . I'll make *sure* it does . . .' I insisted.

He gave me a funny look.

'You know we could just tell my parents. If you think my mum is tough – wait till you see my *dad* get worked up . . .'

I thanked him for suggesting it but still said no.

'We're gonna be like the Scooby-Doo gang,' said Dean. 'Unmasking the demon . . .'

'Exactly . . .' I told him. 'An' by the time I've done with him – he ain't gonna be able to blag his way out either . . .'

'Man – forget that dick who wrote that Hazelwitch book. *We* should write 'em . . .' replied Dean.

TWELVE

I got home about half eight in the morning, after telling Dean that I needed to do a load of stuff. His mum made me stay long enough for breakfast and made porridge, bacon, scrambled eggs and toast. By the time I got out of Dean's house I was stuffed. I walked down to the main road and round the corner to my own street. It was cold and the cars had a layer of frost on them. I shivered as I let myself into the house and the smell of stale booze and cigarettes hit me in the face.

The place was a tip again. In the living room were about twenty empty cans of lager, three ashtrays that were so full that the contents had spilled out onto the floor and a load of silver takeaway trays, some of them still half full of Indian food. I drew open the curtains to let some light in, and despite the cold, opened all the windows. Then I removed a load of empty cans from the sofa and one of the ashtrays, and sat down.

I watched telly for a bit and then got up to see if the kitchen was as bad as the living room. It was worse. There was takeaway stuff everywhere and someone had spilt curry on the worktop, all over the chopping board and down the front of one of the cupboards. There was a strange smell coming from somewhere but I couldn't work out where. It was a bitter smell with an edge of bad eggs. I turned and looked in the sink and nearly threw up. Someone had puked in it, all over the dishes, and just left it.

I thought about waking my mum up, to show her what Micky and his mates had done but I stopped myself. She would be tired and fast asleep anyway. Instead I got out some rubber gloves and started to clear everything up. Again. I ran the tap and tried to let as much of the puke rinse away as I could. It took a while and there were bits of food in it. I nearly added my own vomit to it twice but managed to hold it back both times. Then I washed off the dishes in the sink, glad to see the last bits of puke disappear down the plughole.

By the time I'd finished tidying up Micky's mess it was nearly eleven and I realised that I hadn't decided what I was going to wear to Suky's house. I went up to my bedroom and rooted through my clothes, most of which needed to be washed. I grabbed my uniform and two shirts and put them in an old basket that my mum used for laundry – not that she had done any recently. In the bathroom I found a load more stuff, most of it my mum's and Micky's. I sorted through it and separated my mum's stuff, which was mainly underwear, from Micky's dirty clothes, which I threw back on the floor and stood on. I found a pair of his boxer shorts lying on the floor too and, using the end of the loo brush, I picked them up, opened the bathroom window, and threw them out. They caught on the wind and flew over into the neighbours garden, landing on their dustbin.

Back downstairs I opened the washing-machine door and shoved the clothes in. But then something caught my eye. I saw a pair of women's knickers that were way too big to be my mum's. From doing the washing all the time, I knew my mum was a size ten. These pants were huge – definitely not my mum's, although I didn't want to check the size of them. And then I found a huge bra too, which was a dirty grey colour, but I think was supposed to be white. I stopped what I was doing and looked at them, wondering who they belonged to.

That was when it hit me. Micky was having an affair. He had to be.

I found a plastic carrier bag and shoved the strange underwear into it, ran upstairs and hid it in my room. Then I went back downstairs, just before Micky walked into the kitchen behind me.

'What you doin', yer freak?' he yawned.

'Clearing up your mess,' I told him.

'Good . . . 'bout time you started earning yer keep . . .' he said.

'Have a good time with your *mates*?' I asked.

He opened the fridge and pulled out a can of lager, opened it and took a big swig. Then he belched and farted at the same time, the dirty scumbag.

'None of yer business . . .' he replied.

'Will be soon,' I mumbled.

'You *what*?'

'Nuttin',' I replied quickly.

'Better not be . . .' he said, heading into the living room.

I put the powder in the washing machine and turned it on. Then I stood and thought about what I had just found. I couldn't believe that Micky was so sly that he'd been inviting some other woman round when my mum was at work. I started getting angry at first but then I realised that I didn't have any proof apart from some underwear, and Micky could probably blag his way out of that. He was good at it. I had to find more proof. I stood and thought about how I was going to do that for about half an hour, only stopping when Micky walked back into the kitchen.

'You mad or summat?' he asked.

'Huh?'

'I said are you off yer head, son? Standin' around like a statue . . .'

'Just thinking,' I replied. 'You know that stuff *you* could do if you *had* a brain . . . ?'

For a second I thought that he was going to hit me but he just stood where he was, scowling.

'I ain't got no time for you today . . . just keep out of my way,' he snarled.

'Yeah, whatever . . . just go clean yer teeth, you gum disease ridden rat . . .' I said, quietly.

'*WHAT*?'

'Something wrong?' asked my mum from the door.

I looked at Micky and grinned. He glared at me for a second or two longer and then turned to my mum with his stupid grin.

'Oh, no . . . Just a joke Jit was tellin' me. Ain't that *right*, son?'

I shrugged. 'If yer like,' I said, before turning to my mum.

'What time did you finish last night?' I asked her.

'About six, this morning,' she said.

'You must be knackered . . . go back to bed.'

She shook her head through a yawn.

'Can't. I'm goin' up town with a friend at two. Got to get a dress for a party,' she told me, looking around the kitchen. 'You cleaned up in here?' she added.

I nodded.

'*Ahhh* – aren't you a good lad . . . you didn't have to. I would have done it later.'

'Nah – it's OK. It was like a pig sty in here . . .' I said.

'Yeah – sorry 'bout that son,' said Micky, jumping in quickly, 'that was me mates. I'll give 'em a talking to later.'

'No problem,' my mum told him. 'It was a *party* . . . these things happen . . .'

I didn't reply. Instead I walked out of the kitchen and went and sat on the sofa, changing the channel from some racing programme to a kid's thing. Micky came in after me.

'I were watchin' that,' he told me, as my mum came and sat down next to me.

'*So?*' I replied. 'Now *I'm* watching *this* . . .'

'*Jit*,' warned my mum.

'*Well* – ain't he got a job he can do or summat ; . . ?' I asked.

'That's not fair,' began my mum, only for Saint Micky to step in.

'It's OK, love . . . He's not harmin' nobody. No problem . . .'

My mum said something about Micky being really good with me, and that was it. I threw the remote at the TV and stormed off to my room.

I came down again around half past three and Micky was asleep on the sofa, snoring. He'd already had a few cans of lager and fallen asleep in front of the racing on the telly. There was a newspaper open and one of the ashtrays was nearly full again. I overcame the urge to kick him in the head as he lay there and instead I did what I had planned whilst I'd been in my room. Moving around the room quietly, I looked for his mobile phone, which I found in his jacket pocket along with a tenner note. I pocketed the money and took his phone into the kitchen. I opened the back door and went into the yard, wondering if the neighbours had found Micky's boxers yet.

The phone's battery was low so I opened it quickly and checked his 'calls received' file. There were a load of names on there, one or two belonging to women, but I still had no proof. I switched into his text message inbox and scanned that instead. As soon as it opened, I saw her name. Tracey. There were about twenty messages from her, broken up now and again with ones from my mum and a few other people. I read the last message, which had been sent earlier that morning: 'thnx 4 lst nite. Shme I had 2 go so erly. xxx'

I looked through the living room window and saw that Micky was still asleep. Next I went into his 'sent messages' file. I found a text Micky had sent to Tracey the night before, telling her that the coast was clear. I rechecked his inbox and read some of the others Tracey had sent, realising that I had been right. As I stood and thought hard about what I'd found out, I had a brainwave. Back indoors, I grabbed the landline phone and dialled Dean's number. Micky stirred a bit, mumbled to himself and went back to snoring.

'Got yer . . .' I said quietly.

THIRTEEN

Dean told me to be quiet as I walked through into his parents' kitchen.

'Gramps is asleep on the sofa and if you wake him up he's gonna complain all day.'

'OK,' I whispered.

Dean closed the kitchen door behind us and asked me if I wanted a drink.

'You got any juice?' I asked.

'You kidding? I got orange, cranberry, pineapple, orange-and-pineapple, red grapefruit, grape . . .'

'That's a whole heap of juice, bro.'

'It's my dad – he loves his juice – only drinks that and water. And the odd brandy now and then.'

'Er . . . I dunno which one to have . . .'

Dean grabbed the cranberry and orange cartons and made me a mix of the two.

'Try that man. It's rude . . .'

I drank the mix and said that I liked it as Dean poured himself some. He took a swig and then asked me if I was *sure* that Micky was having an affair.

'Definitely. I found some underwear that don't belong to my mum,' I said.

Dean screwed up his face.

'You know what? I'm a bit freaked out by the fact that you know what size underwear yer mum wears . . .' he said.

'If you did any housework, you wouldn't care less,' I replied.

'Yeah, but you gotta admit it's not normal,' he continued.

I shrugged. 'I ain't embarrassed. My mum is always busy so I do the washing. Ain't no big deal . . .'

Dean looked away.

'I don't mean to take the pi—' he began.

'It's OK,' I told him. 'I don't mind . . .'

He took another swig of his juice before he spoke.

'So, you found some underwear and a load of texts . . . ?'

'Yeah . . . some of them are really nasty too . . . you know, explicit and that?' I told him.

He nodded.

'So, did you bring the sim card?' he asked.

'Nah – I brought the whole phone,' I replied, pulling it out of my pocket and putting it on the table.

'You knob! What if he misses it?' said Dean.

'He won't. He's out cold. And he's always losing his phone anyway . . .'

'Well let's take it to Raj at the phone shop,' said Dean. 'That way you can get it back to him and he won't suss.'

I handed him the phone.

'Check it out for yourself,' I told him, 'though the battery's a bit low.'

'No worries – I can use my charger with it if it dies,' replied Dean, reading through the messages.

'Man, some of these texts *is* nasty . . . nah!!' he said after a few minutes.

'Can Raj copy the sim card then?' I asked, not wanting to reread the messages. They had made me mad enough to begin with.

'Yeah – I rang him. He said to bring it in anytime . . .'

'So, let's go then,' I said, getting impatient.

I wanted to get it out of the way so that I could tell Dean about my new plan to get rid of Micky. The old one had been good but the new one was better and I wanted to run it by my best mate.

Dean got up and finished his juice.

'Ain't this gonna change your plan to get rid of him?' he said, putting his glass down.

'It's gonna make it easier,' I told him.

'How?'

'I'm gonna catch him, bro . . .' I replied.

'What, bumpin' uglies with the whale?'

I nodded.

'Rather you than me, geezer. Even thinking 'bout it is making me feel sick . . .'

'It's the best way,' I said. 'My other plan was too dangerous . . . this way isn't and the others don't have to get too mixed up in it . . .'

'True . . .' agreed Dean.

'I've just gotta work out how,' I told him. 'But let's go do this phone thing first.'

'Come, then,' he said. 'Let's go see the phone man, Stan . . .'

I got back home about an hour later, with Micky's phone and an extra sim card. Raj had transferred all the data from Micky's card over to the new one using a software programme, and I asked him to keep a copy on his hard drive too, just in case I lost mine. I felt a bit like a secret agent, sneaking back in quietly and replacing Micky's phone so that he wouldn't know it had been missing. I was half expecting some bald man carrying a big white cat to turn up and tell me that I was going to be killed, like in those James Bond films that I watch on telly every Christmas.

As I was putting it back the text alert sounded and I was sure Micky would wake up but he didn't. He stirred, mumbled something, farted twice but kept his eyes closed. The message was from his secret woman so I read it. It was a list of days and times, like a rota for lessons or work. Monday 10–3, Tuesday 9–2, Wednesday 12–2 – that sort of thing. It took me a few minutes, after I'd replaced the phone, to work out what the message meant. The woman, Tracey, was telling Micky when she was free during the week. I wondered if Micky was going to see her or if she was going to come to my mum's house. And then I realised that the latest text had helped work out my new plan for me.

I grinned to myself, turning to watch Micky sleeping on the sofa. I crept over and tried a few of the beer cans. One of them was half full. I picked it up, saw his dirty, smelly trainers sitting on the floor, and tipped the lager into them. Then I placed the can so that it looked as though it had been knocked over. I didn't mind the carpet getting soaked either. It would be worth cleaning it up, especially once the dick on the sofa was out of my mum's life and mine, for good.

I'd arranged to meet Suky near Grace's house, outside a bookshop called Browsers. As I was waiting I looked at my reflection in the shop window over and over again, hoping that I looked OK. I had on my one pair of smart trousers and a blue shirt, which I hadn't worn for about a year. My shoes were the same ones I wore to school but I was hoping that Suky wouldn't notice.

As I stood there, looking at myself, the lady who owned the shop, smiled out at me. I looked away really quickly, feeling embarrassed. When I looked back, she was at the till wrapping a book with a bright green and orange cover for some woman. I recognized the book – it was by a local author who had gone to our school years before. Not that I'd read it – books were for girls.

'You thinking of buying something?' I heard Suky ask me.

I turned and smiled at her. She looked really nice, all done up and that.

'Er . . . no. I ain't into books, really,' I replied.

'You should be,' she told me. 'They've got some wicked ones in there . . .'

'Whatever . . .'

Suky smiled and told me that we would walk back to her house.

'Cool,' I replied.

'You're not too nervous, are you?' she asked me.

I shrugged.

'It'll be fine, Jit . . . just smile and answer their questions.'

'Do I . . . er . . . do I look OK?' I asked her.

'You look fine, Jit. Don't worry about it . . .'

'It's just that my mum has been really busy at work and she didn't have time to wash my other clothes and . . .'

'Jit . . . honestly, you look fine. Stop being such a worrywart about it. Relax and that way we can have a bit of fun,' Suky said.

'Fun?' I asked.

'Yeah . . . I feel quite naughty about it . . . conning my parents.'

I shook my head. 'And how you gonna feel when they catch you out?'

'They won't – stop being such a girl about it.'

'Your funeral,' I told her.

'Oh shut up!' she said with a grin.

We crossed the road just past where Grace lives and walked up towards Suky's house. At the first junction we went right into Dovedale. Suky's house was at the top and we walked slowly towards it, as Suky went over who was going to be at her party and apologised for her grandmother.

'I ain't even met her yet,' I said.

'Don't worry,' grinned Suky, 'you will.'

'You make her sound like a lunatic.'

'She is,' replied Suky. 'Right, this is it. You ready?'

I straightened my clothes and nodded.

'Here goes . . .' she said, leading the way.

FOURTEEN

I walked into the hallway behind Suky, realising for the first time just how big her house was. There were rooms off to both sides of the hall and a stairway in the middle. I could hear loads of noise coming from the back of the house and every few seconds a couple of little kids ran in and out of the rooms, chasing each other.

'They're all in the dining room and kitchen,' Suky told me.

'Oh, right . . .'

'I'll take you in,' she said, before pausing. 'In a minute.'

'See? *You're* all worried about it now,' I said to her.

'Sshh!' she said. 'Someone will hear you.'

'Hear him say what?' came a deep voice from behind us.

I turned to see a tall Asian man standing in the doorway, wearing a tracksuit and trainers. He was massive. I felt my stomach turn over.

'Hi, Dad!' said Suky. 'He was just talking about being nervous. Isn't that right Imi . . . I mean Jit?' she said, correcting herself quickly.

'Er . . . yeah. I was . . . feelin' all nervous an' that,' I replied, instantly wishing that I'd spoken in a posher voice.

'No need to feel nervous, son,' said Suky's dad, holding his hand out for me to shake. 'I'm Randeep.'

I took his hand and tried not to wince as he squashed it tightly in his.

'I'm Jit . . .' I replied.

'Jit what?'

'Huh?'

He grinned at me and put his arm around my shoulder.

'What's your surname, Jit?' he asked.

'Er . . . Kooner. Jit Kooner,' I replied, sounding like a knob head.

'Well, Jit Kooner – it's good to meet you at last . . .'

'You too, Mr—' My mind went blank and I couldn't remember Suky's surname even though I'd seen it loads on her schoolbooks and stuff.

'Moore,' he said. 'It means "peacock" in Punjabi . . .'

Suky groaned.

'*What* – and *James Bond* in English?' she said to him. '*Dad* – your jokes are so lame . . .'

Her dad grinned at me like a nutter.

'And you know what "Bond" means in Punjabi, don't you?' he asked.

I grinned back. In Punjabi 'Bond' means 'arse'. I nodded.

'No need to tell you another one of me jokes then, Jit,' said her dad.

'No, there isn't, Dad,' Suky told him.

'Well best go meet the family, son,' he said. 'Mind you, some of them are a bit weird . . . but don't worry. I'll make sure you're all right . . .'

My stomach turned over again, as Suky's dad led us into the dining room, just as someone put on a bhangra tune. I looked around and saw that the room, which was longer than my mum's entire house, was packed full of people and they all stopped to look at me. I stood where I was, frozen, wishing that I hadn't said I'd help Suky out. I was bricking myself.

'Everyone,' shouted Suky's dad. 'This is the mysterious Jit!'

Some people started whispering to each other whilst the rest of them stood where they were, watching me. I didn't know where to look so I looked down at my feet.

'Come on, Jit,' said Suky's dad, 'let me introduce you to a few members of the family.'

I looked at Suky who went red and walked over to a young Asian woman. It had to be her mum because they looked so alike.

'Mum, this is Jit,' she said.

Her mum smiled at me and walked over.

'Hello, Jit,' she said. 'I'm Suky's mum.'

I held out my hand but she grabbed me and gave me a hug instead.

'Yeah . . . er . . . hello,' I said, wishing that she'd let me go.

'Lovely to meet you. Suky has told me all about you,' she said.

'Er, yeah. Me too,' I replied.

'She didn't tell me that you were so handsome though.'

I felt myself going red and looked down at my feet again.

'*Tina*, you've embarrassed the poor lad,' said Suky's dad.

'Oh he's OK,' replied Suky's mum. 'Aren't you, Jit?'

'Yeah – I'm fine,' I replied, wishing that someone would come and rescue me.

'Come on, Jit – let's go and talk to the men,' said Suky's dad. 'Bloody women will have you talking about clothes and make-up.'

'*Dad*!' complained Suky.

'Oh don't worry, Suky,' he replied, 'we won't keep him too long.'

He looked at me and winked.

'We're just going to have a little chat – that's all. Man to man, so to speak . . .'

The knot in my stomach twisted around on itself as I got myself ready to do a runner. I was convinced that I was going to get caught. In one of the corners, a short man in a turban made a whooping noise and turned the music up. Suddenly everyone went back to whatever they were doing, as Suky's dad told me that we were going to the conservatory.

'That's where most of the men are,' he said.

'Er . . .' I said, following him past a load of grinning women and lots of kids.

'You don't say much, do you,' he said. 'Then again – my girl can talk for England. I bet you don't get a word in . . .'

I just nodded, trying to remember what Suky had said about my family. The stuff that I was supposed to remember. Suky's dad told me to sit down at a table in the conservatory and introduced me to his brother, Mandeep, who was older and shorter than he was. He had really bushy eyebrows and hair coming out of his nose, and he was wearing a suit with a waistcoat. The bit of hair he had on his head was in a comb-over. He looked like a cartoon character.

'Lovely to see you, Jit,' he said, in a heavy accent.

'Er . . . yeah,' I replied for about the sixth time. I didn't know what else to say though.

I crossed my legs under the table and then uncrossed them, trying to get comfortable. Suky's dad handed me a glass of juice and sat down too, so that I was stuck between him and his brother.

'What your dad doin' then?' asked Suky's uncle.

'Er . . .'

'His surname's Kooner, Mandeep,' said Suky's dad. 'Bet we know the family . . .'

I gulped down a load of air.

'Kooner eh? I think I know most of the Kooners in the city . . . what your old man do again?' repeated the uncle.

'Owns a load of shops,' I said, quickly, following Suky's story.

'Yes,' said her uncle, impatiently, 'but what him sell?'

I picked up my juice and took a long drink. Long enough to try and come up with an answer. Suky hadn't told me anything about what my imaginary family did.

'Er . . . fried chicken shops,' I told them, saying the first thing that came into my head, mainly because someone had just dumped a big plate of tandoori chicken on the table I front of us.

'*Fried chicken* . . . ?' said Suky's dad, looking puzzled.

I looked away, thinking that I'd blown it already.

'I didn't realise it was fried chicken . . .' he continued, as I waited for him to go mad and ask me who I really was.

'I thought Suky told you what his old man doing?' asked the uncle.

'Nah – she just said shops, that's all. So where are they then?' asked her dad.

I went to grab for my juice, needing to buy more time, but I didn't get hold of the glass right and I sent it flying off the table. It made a loud noise as it smashed against the white tiles on the floor.

'WHOOPS!' shouted Suky's dad.

'I'm sorry . . . !' I said, expecting him to go mad.

He gave me a funny look. 'It's only a glass, son,' he told me. 'But it must be embarrassing . . . first time round here an' all?'

I nodded. 'Yeah – I suppose it is,' I agreed, thinking that Suky's dad was a bit of a joker, and liking him for it.

'Let me get one of the kids to clean it up and get you another one,' he said.

After it had all been sorted out he asked me if I wanted a lager. I said that I didn't drink it and he looked a bit surprised. He opened a can of lager for himself and poured it into a glass.

'Well, it's here if you want it,' he told me, nodding at the glass.

I was hoping that he'd forgotten about the fried chicken shops but he was only just getting started. His brother came back over too, after getting another whisky and Coke.

'So whereabouts are they, these shops?' asked Suky's dad. 'Only you never said because you was too busy making a mess, innit?'

'I think they're all over the place,' I said, wishing I hadn't straight away. It was a dumb answer.

'You *think*, boy? Don't you know where your own father's shops are?' asked Suky's uncle, in Punjabi this time.

I decided to rescue the situation if I could.

'Er . . . no . . . yeah I know where they are. They're in Birmingham and Coventry and that . . .'

'*Ahh*!' said her uncle. '*Because* I thought it was funny. I don't know a single Punjabi chicken shop owner in this city. They are all owned by Muslims . . .'

'Yeah,' agreed Suky's dad. 'And I thought I *knew* all the Kooners here.'

'We're *new*,' I said quickly. 'My mum wanted to move here from . . . from near Birmingham. It's nicer here . . .'

'But I think I know most of the Kooners in *Birmingham*, too,' said Suky's dad.

I shrugged. 'Obviously not all of them,' I said. 'You don't know my dad.'

'Might be we do,' said Uncle Mandeep. 'Whassis name then?'

'*Who*?' I asked.

'Your *arse*,' said Suky's uncle, being sarcastic in Punjabi. 'Your dad, who do you think I mean . . . ?'

'Oh right, him . . . his name's Daljit,' I said, telling them the truth. My dad's name was Daljit – he just wasn't the Daljit Kooner I was telling them about.

Suky's dad nodded.

'I know a Daljit Kooner *here* but he ain't got no kids as far as I know . . .'

My heart nearly jumped into my mouth. What if Suky's dad knew my real dad? But then I remembered that he'd said the Daljit Kooner he knew didn't have kids. So it couldn't be him.

'What about money . . . ?' asked Suky's uncle. 'How much he worth . . . ?'

I shrugged again. 'I dunno,' I told him.

'I got great accountant if he need one. Good at hiding from the tax innit?'

I nodded.

'So . . . how many shop he got?' Mandeep continued.

'Er . . . six,' I lied.

'Worth plenty money then!' replied Mandeep. 'He ever wanna do the business, tell him to call me. After all, we all like family now what with you seein' me niece, innit?'

'Er . . .'

'Never mind that old git,' said Suky's dad, grinning. 'He's only interested in money.'

'I don't mind—' I began.

'Yes, but Suky might. She's in there with her mum,' he said, pointing at the kitchen.

'I'll go and say hello,' I said, getting up quickly.

'Yeah, you do that,' said her old man. 'I'll be here when you're ready . . .'

I gave him a puzzled look. 'Ready for what?' I asked.

'To ask for my daughter, what else?' he said, getting all serious.

'I . . . er . . . I think there's been a misunder—' I stammered.

'Only kidding!' grinned Suky's dad. 'You're pretty easy to wind up, kid . . .'

'Yeah . . . sorry,' I said, even though I didn't have anything to apologise about.

And then just to make things worse, I caught the edge of a mat and tripped, stumbling forward into the kitchen, straight into Suky's grandmother. '*Who's this dog?*' she shouted in Punjabi, as I tried to pretend it hadn't happened.

FIFTEEN

I told Suky that I needed to use the loo and she showed me where the one downstairs was, underneath the stairs. I locked myself in, put the lid down and sat, trying to calm down. I waited a few minutes and decided to wash my hands, just in case anyone was listening. The tap was one of those trendy ones that you lift to start, only I lifted it too far and the cold water splashed out, around the bowl and sprayed my shirt. I swore and looked around for tissue. I pulled a load of loo roll off and wiped myself down. Then I lifted the lid to the toilet and chucked it in, as beads of sweat started to break on my forehead. I pulled off some more loo paper and wiped my head with it, then I put the paper in the loo too.

Finally, I washed my hands and wiped them on even more loo paper. Then I pushed the button to flush the loo. The water cascaded into the bowl and started to go round and round. But instead of the water going down into the pipes, it began to rise, slowly. I jumped back and swore again, watching the water rise, convinced that it was going to overflow and flood the room. I started to panic a bit, wishing that I was somewhere else, as the water continued to rise. And then, just as it reached the rim, it stopped. Hoping that it would eventually disappear down the pipe, I pulled the lid down, straightened my hair and clothes and left.

In the kitchen Suky asked me if I was OK and I nodded, praying that no one would discover what I'd done to the toilet.

'Mum said to give you some food,' said Suky, 'you hungry?'

'I'm always hungry,' I said. 'What you got?'

'Usual,' she said. 'Tandoori chicken, fish, pakora, chickpea curry and rice. Samosas too . . .'

I told her that chicken and samosas would be cool and she put some onto a plate for me.

'Come on – we'll go and eat in the dining room,' she said.

'What – with everyone else?' I said, in a panic.

'Yeah . . . why?'

'Er . . . nothing. Your granny won't be there, will she?' I asked.

'Yeah, most probably. Don't worry – like I said, she's nuts. No one pays her much attention,' said Suky, trying to make me feel better.

I shrugged. 'Go on then – but how long have I got to stay?'

She shook her head.

'For a while, yet. You've not been here long . . .' she told me.

'Yeah but I've shown my face,' I protested.

'Come on, Jit!' she whispered, angrily. 'You said you were going to help me . . .'

'OK, then . . . but if we get caught – you're taking all the blame . . .' I told her.

'Fine with me. Anyway, as long as you keep your cool – we won't get caught,' she replied.

Most of her family were eating when we went in and a couple of her aunts told me that I was a handsome boy and stuff like that. Then I sat down at the dining table, next to some kids.

'You her boyfriend?' asked a little girl with really curly hair.

'Yeah,' I said.

'EHH!!!!' she giggled. 'He's Suky's boyfriend!'

Next to her was another girl of about the same age.

'Do you snog her?' she asked.

'You what?'

'Do you snog her?' repeated the girl.

'None of your business,' I said.

'That means you do!' said the girl, sniggering. 'That's rude . . .'

'Leave him alone,' said Suky, taking a seat next to me.

'Man, does all your family ask rude questions?' I asked her.

'Yeah – sorry about that. They're just inquisitive – that's all,' she replied.

'Like the CIA,' I told her. 'I feel like a terror suspect . . .'

Suky frowned at me.

'That ain't funny,' she said.

'Yeah, I know,' I told her. 'Especially when you're the suspect . . .'

'Just relax, Jit. It's going fine,' she said in a whisper.

I finished my food quickly and went to get rid of my plate but her mum grabbed it from me.

'Let me get you some more, sweetheart,' she said.

'No, that's OK – I'm . . .' I began, but she ignored me and went off to the kitchen, returning with a plate load of chicken.

'Growing boy like you needs his food,' she said.

'Er . . . yeah,' I replied.

'So how did you meet my Suky?' asked her mum.

'School . . .' I said.

'Only she didn't mention you at all until a few weeks ago,' said Suky's mum.

'Yeah – well we was . . . I mean we were all friends and then . . . well . . .'

'We just got together sort of,' added Suky, jumping in.

'Let the boy speak, Suky,' her mum told her.

'It's OK, Mrs Moore – Suky can tell you herself. I don't mind,' I said, looking at Suky.

'It's boring anyway, Mum. It was all "my friend wants to go out with you" stuff . . . nothing too romantic.'

'Really?' replied Suky's mum. 'Shame . . .'

I shrugged and Suky's mum gave me a little smile that I couldn't work out.

'Nice food,' I said, trying to change the subject.

'Thank you, Jit,' replied her mum, grinning. 'Tell me – have you met my mother . . . ?'

'*MUM*!'

'Oh come on, Suky . . . she's a bit senile, not dangerous,' snapped her mum.

'No,' said Suky, 'she's completely off her trolley. Loopy – worse than Grace, even,' she said to me.

'That bad?' I replied, grinning.

'Well, he'll have to meet her, and I don't mean by running into her either,' said Suky's mum.

I glared at Suky.

'I didn't tell her,' complained Suky.

'No – your grandmother did,' explained her mum.

'I'm sorry about that,' I said.

'It's OK, Jit. It happens all the time,' said Suky's mum. 'But she does want to talk to you so when you've finished, pop into the front room and say hello . . .'

I said that I would and returned to my extra helping of chicken.

'I think your mum's trying to fatten me up,' I told Suky, when her mum had gone.

'Yeah – she's still got that Indian thing going on – eat more, beteh,' she replied, making me laugh. Suky looked at me funny for a minute. 'You know what?' she said.

'What?' I replied.

'That's maybe the fifth time I've seen you laugh like that in all the time I've known you . . .' she told me.

I shrugged. 'Lucky you, then . . .'

'You're OK, you know that?'

I grinned. 'You ain't bad either,' I said, through a mouthful of chicken.

'Scratch that,' said Suky, looking disgusted. 'You talk with your mouth full – that's nasty . . .'

Suky's grandmother looked me up and down as I walked into the room at the front of the house.

'Who's this?' she asked in Punjabi.

Suky replied in Punjabi too, telling her my name.

'Jit? Jit what?'

'Kooner . . .' Suky told her.

She cackled to herself, showing the two teeth that she had in her mouth and started going on about some village in the Punjab where the Kooners came from. I didn't understand all of what she said but I got most of it.

'Not as good as us,' she went on in Punjabi. 'Small village, small people . . .'

'Just ignore her,' whispered Suky, in English.

'What?' asked her gran, in Punjabi.

'Oh nothing,' I replied in Punjabi.

'Huh?'

'Sat-sri'Akaal,' I said, in Punjabi, which is how you say hello.

'You speak then, do you?' cackled Suky's gran, before giggling to herself. 'Of course your village is full of monkeys,' she continued.

'Gran!' shouted Suky in Punjabi.

'What do you know, you ugly child?' replied Suky's gran, dissing her. 'You think I don't know that you're swearing at me in your English . . . ?'

I shook my head at Suky.

'Told you,' said Suky.

'Is a good job Imi didn't come himself . . .' I replied.

'Exactly . . . she would have gone mad, I reckon,' Suky told me.

'*Gone* mad?' I asked.

'OK – gone even madder than she is . . .'

'I dunno,' I said, 'she's quite funny in her own way.'

Just as I said that Suky's gran let rip a huge, smelly fart and then giggled to herself some more.

'Nah!!!!!!' I shouted, before laughing.

'Who you laughing at, you son of a cow pat collector?' shouted Suky's gran in Punjabi, which just made me laugh even more.

'That's it,' said Suky. 'Let's go . . .'

We turned to leave and behind us her gran dissed us some more.

'Go on – run away . . . take your son of a monkey with you, you ugly witch . . . !'

I could still hear her cackling from the hallway. I turned to tell Suky that I wasn't bothered by what her gran had said but I didn't get the chance.

'*JIT*!' I heard her uncle shout, pronouncing my name as '*Jeet*'. 'Come and tell me what your father doing. What he worth . . . ?'

I groaned.

'You got me for one more hour,' I told Suky. 'And *that's* it!'

'Thank you, thank you, thank you,' replied Suky. 'You're a star . . . !'

'*JEEET*!!!' shouted her uncle again.

I fought back the urge to do a runner and headed back into the dining room, wondering if Suky's dad would let me have that beer now.

SIXTEEN

I woke up on Sunday in a really good mood. I'd had fun at Suky's house in the end and it gave me a bit of an insight into what my dad's family were probably like. I remembered being at family events when I was very young but they were like dreams. Suky's party had brought it all back, though. I'd even managed to get past another meeting with her grandmother and survive. The problem came when I said I was leaving. Suky's mum said that I should come round for dinner and her dad offered to take me to watch football sometime. I'd nodded and said that I would but now we had a bigger problem. Now that we'd set up the story, we were going to have to stick to it.

And as much as I'd had a laugh at Suky's house – once was more than enough. She'd just shrugged at me and told me that she'd speak to me the following day. And I'd had to give her a kiss in front of her mum to say goodbye too, which was well weird, because I thought about Grace when I did it and felt really guilty. They'd offered me a lift home too but I said no, making up a blag about how

I liked to get as much exercise as possible.

I got out of bed and had a shower before going downstairs into the zoo that was the living room. This time I didn't tidy up. Instead I remembered all about Micky and his other woman and my plan. I kicked a beer can out of my way and went into the kitchen, hoping to find some food. But there was nothing apart from some cold Chinese takeaway and a loaf of mouldy bread. I swore and turned back into the living room. Then I remembered that I'd nicked a tenner from Micky's jacket pocket the day before. I smiled to myself, grabbed my coat and walked the twenty-minute walk to the nearest McDonalds where I got myself a big pile of food.

When I got back in, Micky was sitting on the sofa with a can of lager in his hands and looking rough. He gave me a dirty look and then went back to watching the telly. I ignored him and went into the kitchen to make myself a coffee.

'Mek us one an' all,' he shouted from the living room.

I stuck my head round the door and told him to make it himself.

'You what?' he said, glaring at me.

'I said go make it yourself, you knob . . . I ain't your slave.'

He carried on looking at me for a second or two and then he threw the beer can at me and jumped up. I stepped back into the kitchen as he approached. His face was all red and he stank of booze. He grabbed my arm and pulled me towards himself.

'You little shit . . . who do you think you are?' he spat, the smell of his breath making me feel sick.

I didn't look away this time. Instead I glared right back and told him to eff off. He gripped my arm harder and then pushed me backwards so that I stumbled and fell to the floor. He knelt over me and grabbed my ear, twisting it.

'You need to watch your mouth,' he told me. 'I'm gonna be engaged to yer mam soon and I ain't gonna tek no crap from you, unnerstand?'

I nodded, hoping that he would let go of my ear, which was burning with pain.

'GOOD!' he spat, kicking me in the thigh. 'Now mek me a coffee – there's a good boy . . .'

I was out of the house an hour later, and still hadn't seen my mum. I walked fast, over to Grace's house, angry and scared but determined too. There were tears in my eyes that I wiped away every few moments as I walked. By the time I'd reached her house, they had stopped and I knocked on her door. Her mum answered, telling me to come in out of the cold. 'It's freezing out there, Jit,' she said to me. 'And you've not even got a jacket on!'

'I forgot to put it on, Mrs Parkhurst,' I lied.

I hadn't even noticed the cold until she mentioned it. Looking down at my hands, I saw that they were red and frozen.

'Are you OK, Jit?' she asked, looking concerned. 'You look like you've been crying . . .'

'I'm fine – honestly. It's just a bit windy, that's all and it makes my eyes water . . .'

Grace's mum gave me a funny look and was about to say something else when she saw the look on my face and stopped herself.

'Go on downstairs,' she said. 'I'll get Madam for you. And if there's anything you ever want to talk about, Jit, just ask me – OK?'

I nodded.

'OK?' she repeated.

'Yes – thanks, Mrs Parkhurst,' I mumbled.

Grace joined me in her cellar about five minutes later. I'd been knocking a few balls around on the pool table and trying to calm down. I didn't even know what I was going to say to her. I just had it in my head that I needed to tell her what was going on. Not just the plan to get rid of Micky but everything else as well. And that was making me edgy.

'What's up?' asked Grace, as soon as she saw my face.

I shrugged.

'And this time – don't lie about it. I want to know,' she told me.

I watched her walk over to me and put her arms out to give me a hug. I waited for a few seconds, hugged her back and then, even though I didn't want to, and it made me feel like a kid, I started to cry.

I told her everything. Not just the stuff about the plan but all of it, right from when I was little. All the stuff about my dad leaving us, which my mum had told me, through to Micky turning up, the drinking, the lot. And when I'd finished, I made Grace promise not to tell anyone unless I asked her to. She just sat and looked at me, all sad and upset.

'Why didn't you just tell someone?' she asked me. 'The teachers at school or my parents? Just someone . . .'

I shrugged again.

'All those times that you got into trouble and just walked out of lessons – we thought you were just being rebellious. Hannah told me that you'd been like that since you were little . . .' she said.

'I know . . .' I replied.

'We could tell my parents now,' she said.

'No!'

'But Jit . . .'

'I don't want you to. You promised . . . and anyway, I've got a plan to get rid of him now . . .'

'What's that?'

'I'm gonna catch him with the other woman – get evidence. That's what I need to speak to Imi and Suky about. I need to borrow a camera.'

Grace looked up and half-smiled.

'Let me ask my dad,' she said.

She went upstairs and for moment I thought that she would tell him everything. I started to panic but then I stopped. Inside I knew that she wouldn't say anything. I was just being paranoid. She came back down a few minutes later and shook her head.

'It's at his partner's office,' she told me. 'They're using it all week – sorry.'

'No worries,' I told her. 'Imi said he'd got one so I'm gonna ask for that . . .'

Grace raised her eyebrows.

'Will he do that – lend it to you, I mean?'

I grinned, feeling much better than I had done in ages.

'After what I went through last night at Suky's?' I replied. 'You better believe it, Sister Gee . . .'

Grace smiled wide at that.

'Ooh – call me that again,' she said. 'In a French accent, this time . . .'

'Huh?'

'Only kidding,' she said, leaning over and giving me a kiss on the cheek.

'What was that for?' I asked.

'Just because . . .' she replied. 'Now let's call the lovers, tell them to get their stinky bums over here, and I'll kick your fat ass at pool whilst we're waiting . . .'

'You can try . . .' I said, grinning even wider.

Imi was a bit funny about lending me his brand new camera until Suky told him that they owed me a favour. He nodded and handed it to me, telling me to be careful with it.

'No problem, bro,' I told him.

'It cost over three hundred quid,' Imi told me.

'Yeah – I said I wouldn't break it or nothing . . .' I replied.

'You better not.'

I thanked him and then told them a bit about what had been going on with Micky. Not everything that I'd told Grace but all the important bits. Suky shook her head as I told her and when I'd finished she held my hand.

'That's horrible,' she said, only I wasn't looking at her. I was too busy watching Grace, who looked surprised or angry or something. I couldn't work it out.

'No need to steal his hand, is there?' Grace said to Suky.

Suky looked at her like she was mad. 'What?' she asked.

'You *can* let go of him . . .' repeated Grace.

Suky grinned.

'Me thinks someone's jealous . . .' she joked.

'No, I'm not . . . you're just smothering him, that's all . . .' replied Grace.

'Oh grow up!' said Suky.

'Smelly gimp . . .' said Grace, only now she was smiling.

'Moo!'

'Witch!'

I looked at them both and shook my head.

'Leave it out,' I told them.

They looked at each other and started giggling.

'Shut up, you weirdo!' they replied together, like they were twins or something.

I looked to Imi for support but he had a serious look on his face.

'You sure about this plan?' he asked.

'Yeah – why?'

'I just don't get why you can't tell your mum, show them text messages . . .'

'She's thrown him out three times before but she always takes him back,' I told him. 'It's like she's blind to what he does and that.'

'Yeah, but,' began Imi.

'Yeah, but nuttin'. She needs to have the evidence right

there in her face,' I said. 'It's the only way she'll really believe it . . .'

'If you say so,' replied Imi, ''cause you'll get into trouble at school.'

'I'm already in trouble,' I told him, remembering that I was going to have to face Mr Singh the next morning. 'What's a bit more trouble gonna do?'

Imi shrugged and told me that I was mad.

'Maybe,' I told him.

Maybe I was – but I didn't care. Micky was on his way out of my mum's life, whether he liked it or not. That was just the way things were going to be.

SEVENTEEN

Mrs Dooher waited until she'd finished reading out the messages to speak to me. I had made an effort to get to school early, just to try and get in her good books but it didn't work.

'Jit – can I see you outside in the corridor for a minute?' she asked.

'*Eh*! *Jit's in trouble* . . .' shouted Marco, one of my class.

'Gonna get his ass whipped, innit Miss?' said Dilip.

'Mind your own business,' replied Mrs Dooher.

'But he's gonna get it, ain't he?' said Marco's twin brother, Milorad.

'*Isn't he* . . .' corrected Mrs Dooher.

'Still gonna get it,' shouted Milorad.

I stood up and gave the twins a death stare. They looked away. Dean stood up too, went over to Dilip and the other lads and whispered.

'Careful . . .' he told them.

'But . . .' began Dilip.

'*But Miss I'm picking my teeth up off the floor*,' said Dean, in a high pitched voice.

Dilip went red and shut up.

'Anyone *else* got summat they wanna say?' asked Dean, looking really angry.

No one replied. Mrs Dooher looked at me and shook her head.

'Come on,' she said, softly.

Out in the corridor she told me what was going on.

'Mr Singh has spoken to Mrs Orton about Geography,' she said.

'What – so I'm gonna have to spend the *whole* first lesson with Singh?'

'*Mr* Singh, Jit, and yes you are,' she replied.

'But . . .'

'It's too late for that,' she told me.

'What's gonna happen?' I asked.

'We have to report all unscheduled absences, Jit. Your mum should have spoken to Mr Singh last week. Now that she hasn't – we're forced to take other measures . . .'

'I'm sorry,' I said, trying to get out of it.

She shook her head.

'Maybe you are but that's beside the point, I'm afraid. We don't want to do this, Jit, but we don't make the rules any more . . .'

I looked down at my feet and tried to think of a way out. Just a small blag to cover my tracks until I could sort out Micky.

'OK,' I said. 'You want me to go see him *now*?'

'No, you can go after registration finishes,' she told me.

I nodded.

'And, *Jit*?'

'Yeah?'

'If there's *anything* going on – anything at all – with home or whatever – now is the best time to tell us . . .'

I shrugged.

'OK – get back inside,' she said.

'Thanks, Miss . . .'

I went back into class and sat down next to Hannah and Grace.

'You *all right*?' asked Grace.

I shook my head.

'What's up?' asked Hannah.

'I think they're about to throw me out,' I told them.

'*Really*?' asked Grace, looking worried.

I shrugged. 'Ain't sure but Miss was talking about taking other measures and stuff,' I told them.

'They have to suspend you first, don't they?' asked Hannah.

'I dunno . . .'

'What are we gonna do?' asked Grace, making me smile a bit because she'd said 'we' and not 'you'.

'I need a story,' I told her. 'Just to cover me until I can catch Micky . . .'

'Er . . .' began Grace.

'Your mum's really ill though, *isn't* she?' said Hannah, winking.

'Huh?'

'Your *mum*. She works with mine, doesn't she? And *my* mum told me that *your* mum is off work this week . . .' she continued, winking about four times.

I started to get what she was doing.

'*Yeah* . . . and I need to get home at lunchtime to go *check* on her but I'll be back for the afternoon and that . . .' I said, playing along.

Hannah nodded.

'And I'll *have* to back up any story you tell Miss, or Mr Singh, obviously,' she added.

'*Obviously*,' grinned Grace.

'Right – just act sad,' said Hannah, to both of us.

'*What* you on about?' asked Dean.

'*Just act sad*,' repeated Hannah, 'and tell the lovers to do the same . . .'

Dean leant over and whispered to Imi and Suky. Imi tried to complain but Dean said something else to him and he started nodding. He looked at me and winked. I looked up at Mrs Dooher, feeling bad about blagging her, but I didn't really have a choice.

'Miss?' I said.

'Yes, Jit?' she asked.

'I think there's something you need to know...'

She told me to follow her into the corridor again. Once we were out of the room, I put on a really sad face. Not that I needed to think about it, I was good at being sad for real.

'You know you asked me to tell you summat ... if there was summat wrong and that ...?' I said.

'Yes, and I meant it too ...' replied Mrs Dooher.

'Well ... er ... it's my mum,' I told her.

'Your *mum*?'

'Yeah – she's really, really ill and I don't know what to do and things ain't been right and ...'

Mr Singh looked from me to Grace to Hannah in his office about twenty minutes later.

'And this is the *truth*, right?' he asked us. 'Only you could find yourselves in serious trouble if you're lying. *Serious* trouble.'

'It is the truth,' insisted Hannah. 'Why would my mum tell me lies?'

'Right,' said Mr Singh. 'So what is it you need from me, Jit?'

'Just a few days to get my mum in to see you,' I told him.

'And you need to go home for lunchtimes?' he added.

'Yeah – but I'll be back for lessons ...'

He nodded.

'Your lunchtimes are your own, anyway,' he said to me.

'I know that . . . I just don't want you thinking that I've done a bunk. I thought it would be better to tell you what's happening . . .'

'Well, yes it would,' said Mr Singh.

'So I am.'

'And it took two of your friends to tell me too?' he asked.

'Would you have believed me otherwise?' I said.

'OK – that's fine but you still aren't out of trouble, Jit. As long as you understand . . .'

'Yeah – I do,' I replied.

'And one more thing, Jit.'

I looked at Grace and Hannah, wondering what it was. Mr Singh started to type something out on his computer.

'. . . I need you to get your mum to sign this for me, today, when you go home for lunch. If I *don't* get this from you straight after lunch – the deal's off. Do you understand?'

He hit the print button.

'Yeah . . .'

'Right – get to your lessons and remember – if you're lying to me, I *will* find out . . .'

All three of us nodded and left his office. In the

corridor, Grace and Hannah asked me if I was sure that I knew what I was doing.

'Yeah – I'm sure. I've gotta be anyhow . . .' I told them.

'Why's that?' asked Hannah.

''Cause if I mess up now – you two are gonna get into serious trouble and I'm gonna get thrown out of school . . .' I said quietly.

We walked the rest of the way back to our Geography lesson with out saying another word.

EIGHTEEN

As soon as it was lunchtime I ran out of school and down to the bus stop. The board above the shelter said that the first bus was due in two minutes and the entire journey would take me another fifteen. I stood and waited, hoping that there weren't any road works or anything on the route. I didn't have much time to spare. When the bus arrived I got on and sat downstairs, so that I wouldn't have too far to move when I needed to get off. As each stop went by I got more and more nervous about what I was about to do. What if Micky caught me? What if I was wrong and the other woman wasn't going to be at my mum's house? As I sat and thought about it I pulled out the note that Mr Singh and printed off, got out my pen and forged my mum's signature. It wasn't like I hadn't done it before. And at least this time there was a real reason to do it. A proper excuse.

The bus eventually pulled up at my stop and I ran off and up the main road. As I turned into my road I bumped straight into Gussie, Dean's older brother.

'Easy my yout' – where's the fire?' he asked me.

'Sorry, Gussie . . . I've just gotta get home quick . . .'

Dean's brother grinned at me.

'You ain't gonna make it home if you don't watch where you're goin',' he told me.

'OK,' I said, hoping that he wouldn't ask me anything else.

'So, why you gotta go home anyway?' he said.

'Er . . . just gotta grab summat . . . need it for school,' I mumbled.

'And how's them CDs goin – the ones I gave Dean?' he continued.

'Cool – look I gotta run, man. Can I chat to you later?' I asked.

Gussie shrugged. 'I was only askin',' he said.

I didn't hear what else he said because I looked up and saw Micky and a woman getting out of a battered old car, about a hundred yards up the street. I grabbed Gussie and hid behind him and then let him go and ducked behind a parked car.

'What the raas—!?' he began, but I grabbed him before he could finish and pulled him down to where I was hiding.

'*SSHH*!'

He looked at me like I was mad and then peered around the corner to see what I was looking at.

'Ain't that your mum's house they're goin' into?' he whispered.

'Yeah ... er ... I'll tell you in a minute ...' I told him, watching.

Micky was fishing in his pocket for something and the woman, who had that fake blonde hair and was wearing a short skirt that Hannah wouldn't have got into, grabbed him from behind. He turned, holding the keys, smiled and snogged her.

'Nah ... that's *nasty*,' whispered Gussie. 'That woman belongs on one a dem TV show man ... Obese Britain or some shit ...'

'*SSHH*!' I said again.

I watched them go into my mum's house and shut the door behind them. Then I stood up. Gussie did the same.

'Right ... you gonna tell me what's goin' on?' he said.

'Er ...'

'Who's the geezer?'

'That's Micky ... me mum's boyfriend ...'

Gussie looked shocked. 'An' he's all kissin' up the bog beast pon the street like *that*?'

'Yeah ... I'm trying to catch him out,' I said.

'You done catch him then,' Gussie replied. 'What you gonna do now?'

'Go back to school,' I said.

Gussie gave me a funny look before grinning.

'Tell you what,' he said, 'I'll do yer a deal. I'll ring me mate, Reedy, and get him to drop you off at school, if, on the way you tell me what the *raas* is goin' on . . .'

I looked at Gussie and shrugged. Getting a lift back to school would mean that I'd definitely be on time. I nodded, wondering if Gussie would be useful to my plan.

'Yeah, thanks,' I replied. 'Maybe you can help me out too . . .'

'You want me to kick his ass?' asked Gussie.

'Nah – not just yet. It's summat else . . .'

Gussie grinned. 'Well you better tell me after I ring Reedy and get him to pick us up,' he replied.

'Won't take long, will it? Only I gotta be back on time or I'm dead . . .' I asked.

'Soon come,' he told me. 'Nuh worry yuhself, bro . . .'

Back at school, my mind was racing. I couldn't sit still in Mr Wilson's Science lesson and twice he told me to stop fidgeting. Dean, Grace and the others wanted to know what was going on but I couldn't tell them until afternoon break. When we did get together, out by the tennis courts, they were more nervous than I was.

'What, man?' asked Dean, impatiently.

'Yeah . . . tell us what happened,' added Hannah.

I grinned at them. 'We caught him . . . me and Gussie,' I said.

'*Gussie?*' said Dean in surprise.

'Dean's brother?' added Imi.

'Yep – I bumped into him on my street and we saw them . . .'

'What's she like?' asked Grace. 'Is she ugly?'

'Seriously rank,' I told her.

'One of them that when they're born, the midwife slaps the mother?' asked Dean.

'Exactly . . .' I replied.

'URGH!' said Suky.

'Yeah,' I said. 'Anyway, I told Gussie all about it on the way back to school . . .'

'Gussie came to school?' asked Dean, looking worried.

'Nah – he got his mate, Reedy, to give me a lift.'

Dean nodded.

'Anyway,' I continued.

'Yeah – let him get a word in,' interrupted Grace.

'*Anyway* . . .' I said again, 'I told Gussie, and him and Reedy are gonna help out with the plan.'

'Huh?' asked Imi.

'Don't worry,' I told them. 'The plan's only changed a little bit. But we're gonna do it on Wednesday . . .'

'*This* Wednesday?' asked Grace.

'Yep . . . I was right – those times were when she's free to see him . . .'

'I don't understand,' said Suky. 'What times?'

'On one of the texts that she sent Micky,' I told her.

'Texts – what texts?' asked Imi.

I told them to shut up.

'Let's just get together tonight and sort it out,' I said.

'At my house!' said Grace, excited.

'Yeah . . . Everyone OK with that?'

They all nodded.

NINETEEN

'OWW!'

I gave Dean a dirty look.

'He's standin' on my foot,' he explained.

'Shut up – they'll hear us . . .' I told him.

Gussie and his friend Reedy were standing right behind us, in the back yard of my mum's house. It was Reedy who'd stood on Dean's foot. And he was about eighteen stone.

We were waiting for Imi and Suky to play their part in my plan by knocking on the front door. But that wasn't for another five minutes. I pointed at the lock on my mum's back door.

'I checked it,' I told Reedy. 'It's a Yale one.'

'Cool,' he replied, pulling out two credit card sized pieces of plastic.

'You sure you can get us in?' I asked.

'Easy,' whispered Reedy.

I moved out of the way and he stood in front of the back door. He took one card and wedged it between the door and the frame, under the lock. The other one went above it. Then he started to wiggle the cards about, trying to push them through. He was pushing them really hard and his face went red. I looked at Dean, who was frowning.

'What?' I whispered.

He pointed back at Reedy. When I looked I saw what he was disgusted at. Reedy's jeans had fallen and his bum crack was showing. I looked back at Dean and shook my head.

'Nasty . . .' I said.

'You're telling me,' he replied.

'Hurry up, nuh man!' Gussie told Reedy.

'I'm goin' as fast as I can,' Reedy replied.

Suddenly, there was a popping sound and the back door was open.

'Is it that easy?' asked Dean.

'Told yer,' said Reedy.

'Man – you ain't never comin' round my house again,' Gussie told him.

'Get lost,' replied Reedy. 'I ain't no thief! My dad is a locksmith and I used to help him and that . . .'

I told them to shut up as I crept slowly into the kitchen, praying that Micky was upstairs with his bog beast. The door into the living room was shut so I told the lads to come in. Then I shut the door as quietly as I could.

'What now?' asked Dean.

'Now we give the other two the signal,' I said.

Dean pulled out his mobile and called Imi, letting it ring three times before hanging up.

'You ready?' I asked them, pulling out the camera that Imi had lent me.

They nodded.

'Cool . . .'

My stomach was turning over and over as I waited for the doorbell to go. I was having last minute jitters but it was too late for those. The plan was up and running and nothing was gonna stop it now. It took about two minutes and then the doorbell started ringing over and over. I listened out for movement from the inside of the house. Nothing happened.

The doorbell stopped ringing for about ten seconds and then it started again. This time I heard a noise from the house, banging doors, heavy steps and then another door, the one at the bottom of the stairs into the living room. It was Micky. I could hear him swearing.

'Ready?' I whispered, grabbing the door from the kitchen.

They nodded. I waited until I heard the front door open.

'One, two . . . THREE!' I shouted and we ran into the living room.

Gussie and his mate ran to the front door, just as Micky

was turning round to see what the noise was all about. The shock on his face when he saw two big lads charging at him would have been mild compared to how he felt when they shoulder barged him out of the house and shut the door on him.

I grabbed Dean and ran up the stairs, taking them two by two. At the top I turned into my mum's room and saw the bog beast lying on the bed, naked. I felt the urge to throw up but I didn't have time. She screamed as I grabbed the camera and started taking photos. Dean was groaning at the sight in front of us but he told her not to move. The woman, Tracey I guess, swore at us and tried to cover herself up with the covers. But I already had my evidence and I told Dean that we were going.

My plan then was to go downstairs, face Micky, show him the pictures and tell him that he had to leave or I'd show them to my mum. It didn't go that way though. When I got to the front door, it was open and Gussie and Micky were scuffling in the street. Micky had answered the door wearing my mum's dressing gown and Gussie had ripped it open. Micky only had on his boxer shorts underneath and everyone in the street was watching the scuffle.

I moved towards Gussie and Micky and told them to stop.

'He called me a monkey . . .' said Gussie.

'You are a monkey, you black . . .' began Micky only he didn't finish.

Instead, he realised that he wasn't fighting with a burglar because I was there, holding a camera and grinning.

'What the hell do you think you're doin'?' he shouted, all red in the face.

I held up the camera. Behind him I could see Imi and Suky watching.

'I got your girlfriend on camera,' I told him.

'You sly, conniving likkle . . .'

'Leave it, you greasy little shit . . . you got a choice. Either you leave right now and take the troll with you or I'm gonna show these to Mum and you'll get kicked out anyway . . .' I told him, as I heard a car screeching up behind us in the street. Probably more spectators.

He swore at me. I expected him to swear a bit more only he didn't do that. He went for me instead. I managed to throw Dean the camera just before Micky reached me, his fist catching me right on the nose. We fell to the floor and I was trying to hit and kick him but my head felt like someone was poking hot needles into it and I was in tears. The robe had come off completely now and Micky was going mad. I could hear other people shouting too. I closed my eyes.

The next thing I knew, Micky had been pulled off me.

I opened my eyes and saw Mr Singh and Mr Black, holding Micky, who tried to punch them. I saw Mr Singh land a counter punch in Micky's ribs. And then Micky was on the ground, in just his boxer shorts, coughing. I got up, holding my nose and saw Grace and Hannah. I couldn't work out why they were there. They were supposed to have been at school, to cover for the rest of us. Had they told Mr Singh everything? Is that why Singh and Black had turned up?

And then I saw that there was someone else next to them, crying. It was my mum . . .

TWENTY

It took about a week for everything to calm down again. Micky moved out of our house the same day, along with his other woman, in her battered old car, with my mum going mad at him and threatening to kill him if he ever came back. She didn't mean it but Micky didn't know that and he looked genuinely scared when she went for him. Mr Singh had to hold her back. Then she went inside and started crying loads. When I joined her, she wouldn't stop saying sorry to me and in the end I had to shout at her to tell her that I was OK and that I didn't blame her for Micky. And since then things have been brilliant. She's even cut down on her drinking which is a start, I suppose.

As for school, Mr Singh got us all together a few days after, along with Mr Black, and they made us tell them everything that had happened. And I mean, everything, right down to the lies that we had told. I told the teachers that the blame for it all was mine. I'd made my mates get involved and I'd made them lie for me. Mr Singh listened as I was talking and at the end he told me that he was still going to have to punish the others, but only to tell them off. It wasn't like they were going to be suspended or anything. Then he told them to leave us alone.

They filed out slowly as I waited to see what would happen. Once they'd gone, Mr Black spoke first.

'You know, Jit, you've been a pain in my backside ever since you came to Devana High . . .'

'Yessir . . .' I mumbled.

'You've lied, cheated, fought, played truant, encouraged your friends to get into trouble and generally been a nuisance all round . . .' he continued.

I shrugged. I could see what was coming.

'But then you decide that our warnings aren't sufficient and that you're going to break the school rules whenever you choose to. This is not on, as I'm sure you're aware . . .'

He held up a brown envelope, as Mr Singh walked back into the room. I looked at him, hoping for some support, but he looked away.

'So, the question is . . . What do we do with you? The obvious answer, I'm afraid, is suspension for a month, followed by a meeting between ourselves, your mother, the governors and social services . . .'

'BUT!' I shouted.

'Now, now, Jit, do let me finish . . . I may be firm but I'm fair with it . . .' said Mr Black.

'But you can't throw me out . . . I was only trying to . . .' I began, only I didn't finish.

'This is a letter that we had typed last Friday, Jit, to inform you and your mother that we were about to suspend you for a month, pending further action . . . It's the last door before the one marked exit and you, young sir . . .'

I gulped down air, feeling sick. It was about to happen. I was about to get kicked out of school. I thought about my friends. Dean and Hannah and the lovers. And I thought about Grace. I could feel the tears beginning to well up inside me, along with the anger. My brain was going haywire . . .

'. . . Have managed, with an act of extreme stupidity it must be said, to pull yourself back from the brink . . .'

I blinked through the tears and thought about what Mr Black had just said. I'd thought that he was going to throw me out, but it sounded like . . .

'. . . And considering the circumstances in which you've found yourself for the last eighteen months, I've decided to offer you a reprieve.'

I looked at Mr Singh, who grinned at me. Then I looked at Mr Black, who smiled and then tore the letter up.

'But . . .' I began.

'No "buts", Jit. You're being given two days' leave of

absence from school to sort out things at home. I've spoken to your mother and she is very happy for you to have the time off. Mr Singh will see you home . . .'

I looked at them both and tried to blink back more tears but I couldn't. I didn't know what to say or what to do. Everything was going fine, which was new to me and I didn't know how to deal with it.

'Thank you,' I managed to say.

Mr Black shook his head.

'No need for thanks, son. Firm but fair, that's all. Firm but fair. Now, go on, bugger off before I change my mind . . .'